B.C. Blues

a Sierra Scott mystery

Sylissa Franklin

B.C. Blues is a work of fiction. Names, characters, places, and incidents are the works of the author's imagination or are used fictitiously. Any resemblance to actual events, locales, or persons, living or dead, is entirely coincidental.

This edition contains an excerpt of the single title novel A Mermaid's Tears. This excerpt has been set for this edition only.

ISBN: 0999482505

ISBN 13: 9780999482506

Printed in the United States of America

Visit Sylissa Franklin's webpage: www.sylissa.com

Books by Sylissa Franklin

Cozy Mystery Series

Emerald Wiles

B.C. Blues

Pearls…for Better or for Worse

Turquoise Tantrums (coming soon)

Romantic Suspense

A Mermaid's Tears

Praise for Sylissa Franklin's novel

B.C. Blues

(the 2nd book in Sierra Scott mystery series)

KATZ... **"A real page turner"**

"Thank you for another great book. It was exciting all the way, hard to put it down. Looking forward to the next one."

Chrystal.... **"Great sequel in the Sierra story"**

"I really enjoyed reading about Sierra's next adventure. I'm glad that her friends are in on the crime solving with her now too. Can't wait to read what they all get up to next time."

To Joy Roberts,
for years of deep friendship and big laughs.
I appreciate you.

"Life is tough, my darling,
but so are you."
Stephanie Bennett-Henry

B.C. Blues

Marcus, hugging his weapon of choice close to his chest, slowly peered down the empty hallway. He could hear his opponent down the hall, pacing in the office break room. He figured he was about 25 feet away. A satisfied smile creased his face. Perfect.

He checked his ammo. Yup. Fully loaded. Only one thing left to decide. How to attack. Ambush? Or wait until his opponent charged him? Hmm. That was chancy. His adversary was 160 pounds, all muscle. Technically, he hoped that shouldn't be a problem. Marcus had faith in the Nerf super soaker that he'd borrowed from the neighbor kids. He'd been watching them use it for the last several days. July in Boise was hot, and multiple 100° days were not uncommon. Plus, his super soaker was nicknamed 'Barrage', and had the capacity of a 30-foot stream. That should slow down Hoover, his Great Dane.

A metal dish crashed onto the break room floor, breaking the silence. Responding, Marcus's finger twitched and accidentally sprayed the wall in front of him with the super soaker. He blew out a quick breath, watching long water streaks slowly ran to the floor. Oh –kay, lets go easy on the hair trigger.

It was after office hours. The employees were gone, leaving Marcus and Hoover the run of the place. Literally. Racing down halls and in and out of offices, Marcus did his best to give the dog plenty of playtime. Tonight, he thought he'd amp up the game with the super soaker. Another crash captured his focus. Oh boy. When Hoover tossed his dog dish around - it only means one thing. He wanted to eat.

There were stories on how this Dane earned his name. Marcus had warned the staff...yet muffins, cupcakes, small bags of chips, and a couple of sandwiches had disappeared during the week. And there'd be Hoover, licking his lips, looking totally innocent, ever alert for anything left unattended in the break room. Marcus glanced down at his Timex. It showed after 6pm and Hoover was getting hungry. Patting down his pockets, Marcus found a couple of salmon treats. These could come in handy.

He held his breath, waiting another minute. The break room went quiet. Too quiet. He crept down the hallway, his weapon ready. *Now or never,* he thought. Reaching the doorway, Marcus jumped into the room, focused on finding a large, furry, tawny colored, goofy eared body to aim at. Nothing. He had just enough time to register surprise as he sensed movement to his left. Next thing he knew, he'd been slammed to the floor. Desperate, he started to roll, dodging oversized dog paws that seemed intent on stepping on his groin. All he could do was curl into a ball.

Hoover let out a deep bark of victory, and slowly laid on top of his master, his bony knees, elbows and ankles digging into Marcus's body. "Okay, okay, you win." Marcus laughed and slid the squirt gun aside. Using all his strength, he wrestled the big dog over onto his side and began rubbing his tummy. "Your mama will be jealous that she's missing all the fun." Most likely, Sierra, his wife, would be dumbfounded to learn Marcus let Hoover stay in the office for the week, much less play here after hours.

Marcus was working on keeping his promises, and to lighten up - not take life so seriously. 'A work in progress', he told Sierra. Their trip to Ireland two months earlier, a vacation that turned into the trip from hell, had been life changing. Having a gun stuck in your face will do that. So does jumping through glass French doors to escape the gun. His back twitched. It seemed like a smart idea at the time, but paying for it ever since. Broken glass is wicked, and he had the scars to prove it. Still, he and Sierra survived, as did their marriage. Life was good.

Despite his misgivings, he gave Sierra his blessing when her friend Joan invited her for a long weekend in Vancouver, BC. Sierra would have gone anyway, but he wanted her to believe it was okay that she went without him. Secretly, it wasn't okay. The fact that she could be in harm's way without him close by made his stomach ache. He trusted her completely. His problem was he didn't trust anyone else. Was he being overprotective?

Absolutely. Did it make sense? Didn't matter, that's how he'd felt since he married her. No matter how much she protested, Marcus, struggled with letting go. She'd called him a control freak. Which hurt. Not true, as far as he was concerned. He just wanted her safe. Preferably closer to home. For her part of the deal, she'd been texting several times a day, as promised, and the extra communication helped relieve some of his stress.

Marcus sat up and started rubbing Hoover's velvet soft ears. His cell phone buzzed. It was Max. Marcus was tempted to ignore the call. Max was Joan's boyfriend, and the two of them had been fighting for the last few days. Max had been calling him for advice, and Marcus kept telling him he didn't want to get involved. Still...Marcus picked up his phone. "Max, for the last time, I--" he stopped. Max was talking fast and not making any sense. "Slow down. Start over." He grabbed at Hoover's ears with his free hand. "They...what? They're where?"

Hoover shook his ears free and waited expectantly. "Call the airline," Marcus said. "I'll grab a bag and meet you at the airport." Marcus struggled a few moments to get to his feet, then scooped up the super soaker and headed quickly towards his office turning lights off along the way. Hoover pranced beside him. "I knew it, Hoover," Marcus said tossing the squirt gun on his desk. He grabbed his keys and Hoover's leash.

"I knew there would be trouble. She's like a freaking lightning rod for trouble." No time to wait for the elevator, he threw open the exit door and starting down the five flights of stairs. Hoover followed right behind him. "Sorry big guy, you're off to doggie day care," Marcus said, as he flung himself downward. "Sierra needs my help. Again."

Three Days Earlier...

Chapter ONE

Sierra leaned over as she tugged at her heavy luggage piece, struggling to remove it from the moving conveyer belt. The weight of it dragged her along a few steps before she could heave it onto the floor. An old soft side case, it was a favorite of hers because of all the pockets. It was gray, which she found horribly boring, so she jazzed it up with leopard print duct tape, applying strips along the top and two more strips of the animal print down the sides.

It definitely made it easier to spot from all the other gray, boring cases. She'd played with the idea of using the zebra print tape instead, but decided that might have been too bright. Along with her one bag, she also had her matching carry on. As for her purse, she carried it messenger style.

As they waited for Joan's second bag, Sierra eyed her friend. The trip to Ireland was two months ago, and so much had happened there. And so much had happened at home since then as well. Sierra believed in counting her blessings. Her marriage was intact. Both thanks to - and in spite of - Joan's involvement. She had solved a murder, found treasure, and survived the cold, wet, windy weather of early spring in Ireland.

And, she reminded herself, she'd fought off a killer. She glanced down at her right hand and flexed it. It was still hard to look at. Not because of the missing tip joint of her ring finger. But also angry, red, scars on all her fingers and thumb, running into the palm of her hand. The skin hadn't completely healed yet, and that would come with time. She was grateful she didn't lose her whole finger. Her hand exercises were still painful to do. The doctor had told her she was lucky. With such a nasty infection that had spread from the deep cuts she'd endured, she could have lost her whole hand. Sierra sighed. At least she was left-handed. Still, it's amazing how much humans use the tips of all their fingers. Her job as a data entry clerk was on hold, at least for now. Time would tell.

Joan was determined to prove to her that no one would notice, and even offered to stick a fake fingernail on the remaining joint. Sierra declined, and kept her nails short and natural for now. And while she agreed with her friend that no one noticed, to her it was very noticeable. Hopefully soon, they'd become scars of a warrior - who won.

She still hadn't shared the real story. Even her family didn't know the truth. She and Marcus let them believe the 'mugging in the alley' tale they'd concocted. And no one - not even Joan - has seen the long, angry red scars that streaked down her husband's back.

Sierra knew Marcus still felt his scars from Ireland as well. Jumping through glass French doors to escape being shot by a crazy woman with a gun had been like the best idea at the time...but several pieces of the slivered glass embedded into his back and hip area required extra attention, removal, and extra stitches. All in all, they'd both survived. Their marriage and small business prospered. And now Joan was treating Sierra to a 'girlfriends shopping trip' in Vancouver, BC. Sierra knew she still felt guilty about nearly breaking up the Scott's marriage. Their friendship had been shredded too, but now was neatly healing. Just like her hand, and Marcus's back.

"Okay, are you ready?" Joan pulled her roller bags up next to Sierra. "The adventure is ready to begin."

Sierra laughed. "Are you kidding? You mean, *this* part of the adventure. Right? I can't believe how fast you threw this together. I still think it's a miracle that Marcus didn't come with us."

Joan offered her a Cheshire cat smile. "It was easy. First, I told him this was an 'all ladies' affair. Then, I told him about my cousin's wedding and how we're helping. He already figured out we're going to be super busy. He knows how I like everything perfect. And then I told him he could come *if* he paid for his own airline ticket, his own room at the Pan Pacific Hotel, his own ticket for the train ride, and his own room at the lodge up at Whistler. He declined."

"That would do it," Sierra laughed. "Lead on. Are we getting a taxi?"

"No way! What's the fun in that? Willow is sending a car. We'll head out front. There should be a driver holding a name card."

"Remind me again, who's Willow?"

"Charles Henry's betrothed." A half hour later, they were still standing out front of the airport, waiting. Joan tried her cell phone again. "No answer, my call goes straight to voice mail." Frowning now, Joan punched in a different number. "This is so strange, Charles Henry doesn't answer either."

"So," Sierra asked, "Charles Henry is your cousin, right?"

Joan nodded, glaring at her phone.

"Why don't you just call him Charles? Or Chuck?"

"Because his name is Charles Henry," Joan answered shortly, still staring at her phone, willing it to ring. "And he's my cousin."

"Well, your name is Joan Marie. Do you want me to-"

Joan's cell phone started chirping. "Yes?" she said, without even checking the caller ID. Her smile dropped from her face. "Oh, it's you. Yes, we're here in Vancouver. Everything is fine. Good bye." She slapped her cell phone into her purse.

"I take it that wasn't Willow," Sierra said.

"No," Joan's face turned stony.

"You are really mad at Max, aren't you? Why? What's happened?" Max was Joan's current boyfriend. They had been a couple for two years. And since she'd already been married twice, with a couple of boyfriends in between, Sierra couldn't help but wonder if Max had reached his expiration date. Perhaps his time was up. "So...how come?"

Joan held her hand up, palm out. "Stop asking. Not talking about it." She glanced around impatiently. "I'm done waiting. Why don't you find us some transportation? I'm ready to go to the hotel. Now."

"Okay. Follow me." Sierra stacked her travel bag on top of her wheeled carry-on, and grabbed the handle. With a quick turn, she wheeled her luggage back into the terminal. Joan had to hustle to keep up with her.

"Where are you going?" Joan asked. "The taxi stand is back where we were in the front of the terminal."

"No need." Sierra slowed just long enough to look back at Joan. "We're not taking a taxi. Keep up." After a couple of wrong turns in the sprawling international airport, Sierra finally spotted what she'd been looking for. She turned to Joan. "This way."

Thirty minutes later Sierra found herself stopping for directions. Again. After exiting the Sky Train at the Waterfront Station, she and Joan now stood on a sidewalk in downtown Vancouver, British Columbia. The sidewalks were filled with people everywhere, enjoying the summer weather that had finally arrived.

"The Pan Pacific is near the water, so it can't be hard to find." Sierra said. "My phone shows it next to the cruise ship terminal. I need to see beyond these tall buildings to get my bearings."

"Oh, please, put that away. I know where we are. This is old stomping grounds for me. And for the record, you will never choose our transportation again." Joan announced, while struggling to keep her weekender bag on her shoulder as she pushed her suitcase two suitcases along the sidewalk. "Ever."

Sierra hid a smile. "Oh come on, taking the light rail from the airport was fun. Admit it."

"Never." Shuddering to emphasize her point, Joan shoved her suitcases over the curb as they crossed onto West Cordova. At least the sidewalks were smooth and clean. The hotel still not in sight.

Sierra continued to study the map on her phone. She'd figured a way to push her luggage with her forearms and hold the cellphone steady. "We should be only about three blocks or so from the hotel." A row of tall, skinny high-rise condos on their left blocked their view of water. "Straight ahead should be Harbour Park. Then we'll have our full view of the bay." Her walking slowed. "Vancouver is beautiful." She sounded wistful. "I think I could live here."

Joan snorted. "You wouldn't last two weeks here in the Wintertime. It's ten times the gray and gloom of Seattle nine months of the year."

"Well, everything has to have a little rain sometime," Sierra countered. "These condos are gorgeous. I wonder how much they cost."

"Starting price? Pretty much a million dollars, give or take."

"No way!" Sierra nearly tripped over her suitcase as she savored one last look. "Hey, wait up. What's your hurry?"

"Honestly?" Joan dropped her weekender bag on the sidewalk. She turned to Sierra, hands on her hips. "I feel like a tourist dragging my luggage behind me. And I'm sure all the locals are staring at me, and laughing." She grabbed her bag and threw it on top of one of her suitcases. She was still frowning as she pushed her luggage forward again, trying to walk faster. "The last time I did this, I was in Venice, Italy. And I didn't like it then, either."

"Hang on a minute..." Sierra had to double step to catch up. "I get it. You want to hail a cab. Fine. But this isn't why you're upset. Talk to me."

Joan kept walking. "I'm worried about Willow. This isn't like her. Charles Henry says she never forgets details. Never. We're here to help her with her wedding. And the fact I can't reach her, or that she hasn't called me back is weird." Her phone started chirping again, then went silent. "And yes, I'm unhappy with Max." She slowed down again, giving Sierra a hard glare. "And, no, I'm not telling you why, so stop asking."

Joan maneuvered her roller cases to another curb when she abruptly stopped short. Sierra, gaining momentum, bumped into Joan. "Sorry," Sierra said automatically. "Why'd you stop?" She followed her friend's wide-eyed gaze.

Streaming out from an alley across the street...were zombies. At least a dozen moaning, groaning, teeth gnashing, blood soaked, brain-eating walkers of the dead. The bodies swayed as they shuffled with an odd, off balanced gait. Clothes ripped in shreds, some of them barefoot, they moved with their arms reaching out, as if looking to grab another victim. They turned as one, and slowly started lumbering toward the women. Sierra was sure she saw a couple of them grinning. She nudged Joan. "I...don't think you have to worry about anyone looking at you."

A young man following behind the zombies came running up in front of them, a small video camera focused on the full group. Sierra could hear him shouting directions. An assistant ran up next to him, waving her hands, leading the zombies toward a nearby coffee shop.

"Welcome to Vancouver, BC," Sierra said wryly, secretly disappointed to see the zombie crowd moving on. "Hollywood of the North."

The doorman welcomed them to the Pan Pacific as they stepped towards the glass doors that glided open for them. He was tall, blonde, and young, and Joan flirted with him outrageously. After a few steps, Sierra realized that the actual lobby was up the escalators. The downstairs area opened into the Convention Center, combined with the lower level with the hotel entrance. Once at the top of the stairs, they enjoyed the full view of the bay through floor to ceiling windows as they shifted with their luggage to the right side of the lobby, and up to the check-in desk. After only a few minutes, they were on their way to the room.

Sierra caught the flash of irritation on Joan's face as her cell phone chirped in the purse pocket. "Aren't you going to at least ask what he wants? That's like the fourth time he's called since we got off the plane."

"I know what he wants." Joan shook her head. "He can wait."

Their room was on the tenth floor and offered an open view of the east side of Vancouver Harbour. Sierra couldn't get over how green everything seemed, fresh blue sky, and lots of warm sunshine everywhere. She finished putting away her toiletries in the bathroom and grabbed her sunscreen. "Hey, I have an idea...since you're so hot on burning calories, let's go rent bikes and check out Stanley Park. Maybe we can find more zombies."

No response from her friend, who was frowning while texting on her phone. Sierra tried again. "We could call the concierge desk and book a dinner cruise." Still no response, and now Joan turned away from her. "All right, you win. Let's get tattoos. I'm thinking we should each get a row of roses across our chests. I'll do purple, you do black."

Joan, still looking at her phone, reached into her bag and pulled out an oversized envelope and handed it to Sierra. Then she walked into the bathroom and closed the door. Sierra heard the lock click into place. Sitting on the queen size bed closest to the window, she pulled out several sheets of paper. It was their itinerary for the long weekend. She blinked. Wow. This was tight. The bathroom door opened and Joan came back into the room. She tossed her phone on her bed.

“Seriously?” Sierra held the papers up at her, eyebrows raised. "I think you're trying too hard. It feels like every minute is accounted for. Is there any time to use the bathroom? Or lie on a chaise lounge by the pool?" Her eyes narrowed with suspicion. "Did Marcus put you up to this?"

Joan blanched. "No." Still, she couldn't look her friend in the face. "I just...wanted Marcus to know he could trust me."

"Trust you?"

"Yes, well, you know. After what happened in Ireland, I promised him we'd be too busy to get into trouble. Or, cause any trouble."

"Or cause any trouble? You mean, like, 'looking for antiques'?" Marcus's cryptic phrase for 'butting into someone else's business'.

"That did come up, yes. I assured him antiques were not on our agenda."

"Exactly what *is* our agenda?" She waved the papers again. "A lot of times and places are listed, but there aren't any details."

"Because that's a copy of the version I gave to Marcus." Joan started ticking off on her fingers. "We're spending tonight and tomorrow night here in Vancouver, helping Willow with final details for her wedding. That takes care of Thursday and Friday. Then, Saturday morning we're taking the Sea to Sky train up to Whistler for the wedding, staying one night on the mountain. Sunday, we’re back here for one more night, then Monday we fly home. See? Pure fun. Lots of time for shopping, eating, sightseeing..."

"Biking?" Asked Sierra, hopefully. She watched her friend roll her eyes. "Oh come on Joan. Stanley Park is gorgeous, right next to the water." No response. "You can ride a bike, can't you?"

"I'm too old." Joan replied flatly.

"What? Since when? You're the one who convinced me to try zip lining. And you're only ten years older than me. Not even forty - yet," added Sierra. "You haven't even reached second adulthood."

"Oh, thank you."

"Hey, your excuse is bogus and you know it. Age has nothing to do with this. So tell me what it is."

Not answering right away, Joan finished emptying her carry on, tucking her hairbrush in her hand and applying a few brisk strokes through her hair. Chin length, her blonde hair was as straight as Sierra's brown hair was curly. Both women loved their thick hair.

"Quit stalling, we're losing daylight here." Sierra eyed her friend closely. "You know, we don't have to do everything together. You can hang out at the bar or by the pool, that's fine with me. I'll just be gone for about an hour. And then I can meet you-"

"No way."

"Well, then?"

"Fine." Joan was not happy. "It's just that I haven't been bike riding since I was eight years old. I'm not sure I remember how, and I'm not real excited about falling down and scraping various body parts."

Sierra blinked. "Wow. Where do I start? First of all, I'm with you on the falling down and hurting yourself part. But trust me, it's easy to remember how to ride a bike. It's a matter of balance. And I promise you, I'll set a slow pace." She grabbed her lightweight jacket, shoving her wallet and hotel key card in the front zipper pocket. "And to prove I'm sincere, I'll buy the first round of drinks when we get back."

~~~

They sat poolside watching billowy clouds above, and boats sailing in the bay below. Both ladies were drinking iced tea. Joan had survived the bike ride, where Sierra had led the way through Stanley Park and along the wharf area. Feeling a bit smarmy, Sierra wasn't ready to let go of the bicycle adventure. "Wasn't it just gorgeous today? That ride felt wonderful, don't you think? You did really well...until you lost your focus and ended up in the pond." She paused to sip her tea. "Is your hair dry yet?"

Joan lifted her sunglasses to direct a glare at her friend. "Enough already. That wasn't my fault. Who dresses up and walks around in medieval costumes? What was that all about? I don't remember everyone in this city being so crazy. And besides, my calves were starting to cramp. Yes, it was pleasant bike ride, until the end. And no, I won't be biking again."

"At least that jogging EMT guy who came to your rescue was cute." Sierra was grinning now. "I love how he jumped right into the water and pulled you out. He even went back in for your bike."

Joan couldn't help smiling. "He was right there on the spot, wasn't he?" She glanced at her watch. We need to get going; I don't want to be late for our meeting with Willow. We're meeting her at Tiffany's, in the Golden Triangle."

Sierra snorted. "Sounds more like the Bermuda Triangle, except your money disappears instead of your plane." Sierra sat up straight. "Wait. Did you and Willow finally connect?" Joan shook her head. "Okay, so tell me how you know her."

"Actually, I don't know her." Adjusting her sunglasses, Joan grabbed her iced tea. "In fact, I've never met her. I have a picture of her that Charles Henry sent me on my cell phone." She took a short sip and made a face. "Tastes bitter," and set the glass down. "My cousin is four and a half years older than me and I adore him. He's my only male cousin. He's also the only one in the family that's never harassed me about my love life. Plus, he's never married. So if he says Willow is the one for him, then I know I will like her."

"Do we have time for dinner before we walk over to Alberni and Burrard?"
~~~

"Only if we start now." Joan swung her legs over the chaise and slipped her feet back into her sandals. "Should we eat surf? Or turf?"

~~~

Dinner finished, they meandered from their hotel. The evening was warm and softly lit with the beginning of a colorful sunset. Stopping a moment Sierra reached into her purse and pulled out her cell phone to take a picture, and texted it to Marcus. The view of crimson and gold reflecting over the bay was breathtaking, and she knew Marcus would be anxious to hear from her. "I'm glad we're walking," she said. She'd wolfed down her fish and chips, along with a couple of bourbon Cokes. There were plenty of calories she wanted to walk off.

Tall office buildings stood in front of them, while the modern million dollar condos lined the waterfront, towards the sea to their right. She'd always lived in a home in a suburban area, needing a car or a bus route to get where she wanted to go. It tickled her imagination to consider living and working in the same area, walking to work, to the grocery store, her favorite restaurants, and home again.

The streets were well lit, and she loved how the city proudly displayed the Canadian flag above their stores. Tiffany's stood across the street from Hermes. And she had no doubt that if they didn't have time tonight, Hermes was on the top of Joan's must-see list for tomorrow. For now, Joan appeared to be on a specific mission.

The downtown streets were filled with just as many people in the evening as there had been in the afternoon, many of them walking their dogs. Watching the owners made Sierra miss her own dog, even if most of her friends and strangers alike considered him more like a horse, or at the very least a pony. Instead, he was a three-year-old 160 pound Great Dane, with a solid fawn color body with undocked, goofy long ears. Danes bodies carried deep chests and heavy muscled front legs, and were often used in Europe pulling small carts. Marcus kept threatening to buy a cart for Hoover, just for the holidays. He liked to envision himself dressed up as Santa, and Hoover decked out in
~~~

red or green as an elf. So far, Sierra had managed to veto the vision.

It took a few minutes, but she realized what seemed...odd. Lots of people were dressed in period costumes. She spotted two groups of people wearing 'Roaring Twenties' theme, others in Renaissance, wigs and all. She stopped to stare at one group that wore total body makeup as 'little green men'. Most groups consisted of four or five people, with at least one in each group holding a camera.

At least there weren't any roaming zombies. She shrugged. Maybe it was a city thing. Or a university thing. Or perhaps something spontaneous. She recalled the weekend she and Marcus were walking through Saturday Market in downtown Boise, and saw a trio of women holding signs offering free hugs. One of the ladies was celebrating her birthday, and a scavenger hunt had been designed for her and her friends. They'd spent the morning all over downtown Boise, doing fun, silly things. It looked like a good time.

At the entrance of Tiffany's, a doorman asked for Joan's name, then asked if either of them carried a cell phone or a small video camera. They showed their cell phones, then tucked them back into their purses. Sierra paused as he opened the door for them. "This is only Thursday night, right?" He nodded. A tall, thin woman with a friendly smile and red hair stepped forward. Dress in black her gold and ruby jewelry stood out. Her earring and necklace, along with a couple of rings, glittered under the stores lights. "Joan, it's great to see you. I'm so glad you called, it's been a while."

"Kris, you look wonderful," Joan gave her a brief hug.

Kris Query turned to Sierra. "Good evening. I'm so glad you could come as well, Mrs. Scott. Would you follow me please?" She motioned them to the back of the store.

Sierra glanced at Joan with raised eyebrows and whispered. "She knows my name...why?"

Joan merely smiled. "We have an appointment. They like to know who's in their store. It doesn't mean you have to buy anything."

Sierra glanced at the jewelry sparkling brightly in the cases. "That's good." Marcus had to know Joan's itinerary included Tiffany's. She didn't plan to buy anything, but still, her policy when dealing with Marcus concerning jewelry was, 'don't ask, don't tell'. The store was by no means empty. There were others looking around as well. But everyone was either in pairs, or in groups of three or more. There were no individuals.

Looking around, she focused on the other shoppers. There were two couples looking at engagement rings. A threesome of older women, each dressed up as 1920's flappers including feather hats, were looking at necklaces. Each taking turns holding a video camera on the others. They oooh'd and ahh'd loudly, rolling their eyes and flashing the rings at the camera.

Another group, two guys and a gal, were looking at loose stones. One of the men also had a small video camera and appeared to be shooting the couple picking out stones. The woman laughed, her smile wide as she turned and caught Sierra's eye. Sierra smiled back. The woman quickly turned away and squeezed the man's arm. Her nails were long, square shaped, and painted an odd matte aqua blue with rhinestones. Sierra glanced at her damaged right hand, curling her fingers into a ball and pushing both hands into her pockets of her capris.

Sierra turned back as Joan showed the clerk a photo on her cell phone. "We were asked to show our phones and not use our cameras. What's with their cameras?" she asked the sales clerk.

Kris rolled her eyes and reached behind her to grab a flyer. She handed it to Sierra. "Apparently there's a big 'Indie Production' contest going on this weekend. We've had several calls for permission to use our store as a set. Corporate doesn't want customers filming in here, but these couples made an appointment before we knew the policy, so we're allowing it tonight. But they're the last allowed in the store. People are welcome to film outside the store, as long as they keep it short, sweet, and it doesn't involve weapons."

"Well, this explains the zombies," Sierra said. Still reading the flyer, she sensed someone walk to the counter and stand right next to her. Looking up, her eyes met a pair of bright blue eyes. Sierra was then drawn to the older woman's hair, which was blonde with gray streaks, cut and styled in a short bob cut. And then her eyes focused on the largest Ceylon Blue Sapphires she'd ever seen. At least seven carats each, the rectangle cut stones were paired as earrings, in platinum, surrounded by at least two-carat worth of white Diamonds. Sierra felt her mouth go dry. She'd kill for those earrings.

The blonde smiled at Sierra's reaction. "Unbelievable, right?" She turned and tapped Joan's shoulder. "Hi, I'm Willow. Are you Joan?"

Joan turned to the taller woman to say hello, but found herself being pulled into a big hug. "Charles Henry has told me so much about you," Willow said. "Thanks for coming and being a part of our happiness."

Joan laughed, the surprise on her face turning into a smile. "It's so nice to finally meet you, Willow. I never dreamed anyone could ever tame Charles Henry."

"Oh, well," Willow said. "What makes you think that? Maybe he's tamed me?"

With that, Sierra, Joan, and Willow laughed. Kris brought out an opened, chilled bottle of sparkling wine and three wine stems. "So tell me," Willow asked. "What did you think of the town car and the city tour? I didn't know if you were a white or red wine drinker, so I requested the service provide a bottle of each, with lunch." She was looking expectantly at Joan; Sierra was wishing they didn't have to tell the truth.

Joan didn't hesitate. "Willow, I'm sorry, I have to tell you that the town car never arrived. We waited a half hour and then found our own transportation downtown."

"Oh, no!" Looking from Joan to Sierra, Willow realized they weren't kidding. "I shouldn't have delegated this. I should have followed through myself. I am so sorry. You must think I'm a total space cadet!"

"No problem," Sierra said quickly. "We had the chance to explore the downtown area ourselves. We took the light rail from the airport to downtown."

Willow's look of total amazement led Sierra to believe that apparently nobody in Joan's family used the light rail. Sierra grinned. "Oh yes, and we pushed/pulled our luggage over to the Pan Pacific." Ready to tell more of the story, Sierra found her open mouth covered with Joan's hand.

"Enough," Joan said. "The champagne is getting warm." Joan and Sierra each took a glass, as did Willow. Raising her glass, Joan said, "Congratulations, Willow. I wish you and Charles Henry many years of happiness."

"I'll drink to that," Willow replied, as each lady sipped her wine. Sierra glanced around the shop, surprised to find it now empty of customers, except for them.

"We're closed now," Kris said, catching Sierra's look. "But we stay open for appointments." She nodded toward Willow. "She and Mr. Bishop are very special clients."

"Charles Henry insisted," Willow said, gently touching one of her earrings. "I can't wear rings, because of my rheumatoid arthritis. My knuckles swell too much." She laid both hands on the glass counter. She shrugged. "Not much I can do about it, so life goes on. But C.H. was determined to give me an engagement ring. So he had the earrings custom made - along with a matching bracelet. That will signify my wedding band. I asked him not to," Willow said quickly, seeing Joan's eyebrows rise. "Don't get me wrong, I love jewelry. It's just a little showy. Especially since this is a second marriage for me."

Sierra liked Willow. The woman's hands were misshapen, and yet she didn't shy away or hide her hands. She obviously didn't care if anybody judged her. "How did you two meet?"

"At one of my yoga classes." She laughed at Sierra and Joan's reaction. "I've been teaching for twenty-five years. It's better than exercise. She fluttered her fingers. I have a private studio behind my house for small classes. In early February, C.H. came to a class with a friend." She leaned in closer to Sierra and Joan. "Actually, I thought his 'friend' was his current girlfriend. But it turns out they weren't very serious."

Willow's face grew pensive. "I'm 58 years old and lost my husband five years ago. I never dreamed I'd find love again." Taking Joan's hand in hers, Willow spoke softly. "I had no intention. None. But C.H. wouldn't take no for an answer." She shrugged again, a shy smile on her face. "And I soon realized, I didn't want to say no."

Joan laughed and nodded. "Oh yes, that's Charles Henry. Once he makes up his mind, there's no stopping him. And let me say, he has excellent taste."

"May I show them the bracelet, and his wedding band?" asked Kris.

"Of course," Willow said. "I added four gems to the bracelet, and the same in C.H.'s wedding band."

Sierra peered at the small boxes that now sat on the small glass table next to the bottle of wine. The bracelet was stunning. Three flowing strands of oval cut Ceylon Blue Sapphires, set in platinum, each stone one-carat. Added to the bracelet were a single Amethyst, white Diamond, Freshwater Pearl, and a Peridot. The platinum wedding band for C.H. held the same four gems, plus a half-carat Ceylon Blue Sapphire. "Wow," said Sierra. "These are amazing. Obviously each gem means something. Can you tell us?"

Hesitating a moment, Willow lowered her head. Then she looked up at Joan. "Since you're C.H.'s best man...and my new friends." She motioned to include Sierra and leaned in closer. "You can't breathe a word of this to Charles Henry. I'm doing this on my own." Sierra nodded eagerly, she loved secrets. "The amethyst is for February, when we first met. The Diamond is for April; he says that's when he knew he was head over heels in love with me. The pearl is for May, the month he first asked me to marry him. And the peridot," Willow tapped the light green stone, "is for August. When I told him, yes."

"You mean, as in earlier this very month?" Joan couldn't hide her amazement.

"Yes," Willow answered. "I know it seems fast, but for us, it feels right."

"Hey, my cousin is happy. I'm sure you'll be perfect for each other." Joan said. "And according to your schedule, Sierra and I meet you around noon tomorrow at your house. We hit the dress shop first, and after that, the bakery. Right?"

"Right." Willow smiled. "If you want, you can join the Friday 6 am yoga class. It's my last one, since C.H. and I are moving right after the wedding. It'll be a full class and you're welcome. I'll be serving coffee and pastries afterwards. Complimentary, of course."

Sierra was about to say sure, but Joan cut her off. "No thanks, your friends and students will want as much time with you as possible. So if it's okay with you, we'll meet you at our original time."

"No worries. I can be ready to leave at noon. Just to warn you, I'm holding an estate sale that starts tomorrow. Hopefully there will lots of people at my house. C.H. thinks I'm crazy to do so much at one time. But I've planned it for weeks, and we've been setting up since earlier this week. I'm trying to sell off as much of my stuff as I can. C.H. and I are moving to Australia, so I'm liquidating as much as I can into cash. It's a big job so I've hired a firm to be in charge of all the advertising, and the estate sale itself. But I need to be there in the morning to sort out a few things."

"I love estate sales," Sierra said brightly.

Joan nudged her and threw her a warning look. "Wow, I knew Charles Henry did a lot of work in Australia, but you're actually moving there? When is Charles Henry due back from Australia, she asked.

"Not until late tomorrow night." She caught Joan's incredulous look. "I know, that makes it Friday night. He's cutting it close. We take the train Saturday morning up to Whistler, and the ceremony is later that afternoon about an hour after we arrive. He better be on time *and* able to stay awake. Brisbane is close to a twenty-four hour flight. Who knows which time zone his body will be in?"

Joan gave Willow a hug. "Don't worry, it doesn't matter. He can sleep after the honeymoon. He's so excited, there is no way he would miss this, not for the world."

"I'm so glad you're here to help." Willow reached out to hug Joan again. She offered a hug to Sierra as well. "I'll see you gals tomorrow, then. This is going to be quite the adventure!"

Chapter TWO

That bitch!" The smile was gone, and unable to contain her anger any longer, the comely blonde exploded with a series of expletives once she settled into the back seat of the waiting car. She had kept up appearances as she sauntered out of Tiffany's and around the corner. There were too many people out and about, and definitely too many cameras. Still, that didn't stop her from shredding the flyer she carried, dropping the pieces as she got into the car.

"Hello, to you, too." Her brother, Rupert, was bored; and tired of waiting for her to 'confirm things', as she put it. He was used to her outbursts. And as long as they weren't directed at him, she could rant all she wanted.

Moments later a wig of blonde, shaggy hair flew into the front passenger seat. He glanced at it as he pulled away from the curb and edged the car into traffic. "Do you think she recognized you?" he asked, careful to keep his eyes on the road. The yelling had stopped, but he could still hear her grumbling.

"No," she growled. "She was too busy making nice with her two new buddies." Another loud string of profanity followed. "I can't believe she's such a liar. She's downsizing, uh huh, moving to Australia just like she said. Oh yeah..."

"But?" Rupert's sister, Gwendolyn, had an annoying habit of not finishing her sentences out loud. He continued driving in silence. It was a busy Friday night, and traffic lightened up once they were out of the downtown area. They were driving back to Willow's house. Gwendolyn's company, Royal Estates Services, had been hired by Willow to help her downsize. They were in charge of taking inventory of all household items, advertising of the sale, marketing the larger items in separate ads, as well as running the sale. Willow was only responsible for packing personal items and setting aside whatever she was keeping for herself.

He gauged the grumbling still coming from the back seat. He'd learned the hard way Gwendolyn needed time to process bad news. He could wait. Now he could hear voices, and realized she was playing back the video. A couple of minutes later, the small video camera flew past his face, startling him, as it landed right next to the blonde wig. He cursed under his breath, one of these days she'd cause him to drive into a tree.

"She's getting married," Gwendolyn spat out, as if the words were bitter in her mouth. "To Charles Henry – *they* are moving to Australia." This had been a weird gig, which had gotten even stranger in the last few days. Gwendolyn was brilliant when it came to marketing. Her clients loved her because she was very good at getting results. She charged a high commission, and she was worth it. She stayed positive and focused with the clients, but this time-things were very different.

Rupert heard the soft rattle of ice, and the soft whish of an opened soda can. Finally. Gwendolyn would soon be approachable again. "Do you want me to drive you to the house, or not?" The plan had been to return to Willow's house and finish setting up for the sale scheduled to start tomorrow. But now? He'd drive in circles if he had to, there was no way he'd ask again.

The car on cruise control, his hand automatically went for the cigarette pack in his shirt pocket. He moved his hand back onto the steering wheel and sighed. It was gonna be a long night. Glancing at the rearview mirror, he caught Gwendolyn's hard stare. Yes, smoking was a bad habit, but he couldn't help it, working with Gwendolyn was turning him into a nervous wreck. He'd tried gnawing on carrots, but the sound of crunching food only enraged her. He felt safer smoking. Go figure. Sighing, he left the cigarette pack where it was.

"Let's go back to the house," she said. "I want to finish up a couple of things. Then we'll head back to Victoria."

"Wait. What? The sale is scheduled to start tomorrow at nine, first thing in the morning. I thought you were planning to sleep in the guest room?"

"Calm down. You really need to learn to be flexible, Rupert. We'll catch the early ferry over and be here in plenty of time." She sat back as Rupert signaled, turning off the main road and back to the neighborhood. It was dark outside, and passing streetlights reflected on both their stoic faces. Gwendolyn's temper tantrum may be over, but her undercurrent of rage felt like a levy being breached by a flood, and about to burst.

~~~

Joan was in a quiet mood as they walked back to the hotel, so Sierra pulled out the flyer and started reading about the Indie Movie contest. "This had to be why the doorman at Tiffany's questioned us. And it explains the zombies, and the costumed people in the park. The prize is a cool one million dollars, and, there's no entry fee."

She looked up just in time to avoid smacking her head into a lamppost. "It can only be three minutes long," she continued, as she sidestepped the pole. "The premise is a choice of: surprise or shock. And it must be filmed within a 16-block radius of downtown Vancouver. Hmm, maybe I'll make a video and enter this contest. How hard can it be?"

"Are you saying you want to film our weekend getting ready for Willow's wedding?" Joan clearly had no interest.

"That's not a bad idea." Sierra caught the stony look on Joan's face. "No, no." Sierra answered quickly. "Too much work. I'm just curious how the public services and park employees are feeling about this, especially after what we've seen. But it's only for three days, and it ends Sunday night. Then people have to mail their DVD to a P.O. Box, postmarked by midnight." She squinted at the fine print. "Winner to be announced in three weeks."

They stopped in front of the entrance of their hotel. The night was perfect. Lots of music, people laughing and walking nearby. The soft breeze was light and warm. Sierra glanced at her watch, it was only 9:30. "It's too early to go to the room. Let's go watch the boats in the harbor."

"You go ahead," Joan said. "I'm tired, plus I have some number crunching to do for tomorrow."

Sierra opened her mouth to tease her friend, but stopped, something was obviously bugging Joan. Hopefully it wasn't too serious. Double-checking that she had her room key, Sierra stood
~~~

on the walkway along the edge of the hotel. Night was coming quickly now, dark blue sky with faint traces of orange and red from the earlier sunset.

"You're a beautiful city," Sierra announced to the water lapping at the pier. "You seem perfect, to me." A half hour later she walked back to the hotel, taking the elevator to their room. She'd claimed the bed closest to the window earlier that day. There was no need to set the alarm, Sierra always woke up early.

~~~

Yawning, Sierra stood in front of the familiar blue water out in the bay. But now the sun was coming up over the mountains of North Vancouver, sending golden sunlight everywhere. Ah, the joy of Pacific Time, it may be six am here, but in Boise it was seven. Walking towards the local Starbucks for her and Joan's morning coffee fix, she couldn't help but appreciate all the green foliage that filled Vancouver.

Once inside the coffee shop, she stood in a short line and placed her order. The barista had just taken her money when suddenly the small shop filled with a surge of people. All of them were dressed up in party clothes. A large man, dressed as a pastor, walked solemnly through the crowd and stopped at the counter. He turned to face the entrance.

Just inside the door, a ten-year-old girl dressed in a sparkly dress of hot pink and wild silver stockings, punched the button on a CD player. Cranked on high volume, the store filled with organ music. It was the Bridal Chorus, the most familiar wedding march. The door opened again, and two men dressed in black suits quickly walked up to the counter and stood by the pastor.

Next came two little girls who looked maybe six or seven years old, walking toward the pastor. Dressed in yellow chiffon, each held a small basket of daisies. Next, a young woman, probably in her late 20's walked in. Also dressed in yellow chiffon with a matching ribbon in her dark hair, she carried a bouquet of daisies. She stood on the other side of the pastor; the two flower girls huddled close to her. Now everyone in the shop shifted their gaze toward the door.
~~~

The bride, her brown hair braided and entwined with white mini roses, was short and a little heavyset, her bosom threatening to spill over her strapless wedding gown. All in white, her veil twinkled with sequins and added a sparkle when she walked. She was smiling, clearly in love, and looking only at the groom. Her bouquet held white roses, with daisies mixed in. Sierra couldn't help but smile.

A weird place for a wedding, but hey, it was romantic. She grabbed the coffees, and sipped on hers. Everything had come to a halt, and it wouldn't be until after the wedding that anyone could leave.

Sierra glanced at the barista behind the counter. Uh-oh. No one was taking orders, the staff members were watching the wedding. She glanced around at the customers standing behind her. They were not so happy. She also noticed two people holding cameras. One focused on the wedding party, the other one was focused on the crowd. She kept a smile on her face. Was this event for one of those videos being made for the million-dollar prize? Sierra had to give the bride and groom credit. They kept the wedding short and sweet, and five minutes later, Sierra and other wedding guests were walking out the door.

~~~

"Okay, tell me again why I'm eating eggs for breakfast?" Joan was frowning as she poked at her mushroom omelet.

Sierra sighed. Joan had no interest about the impromptu wedding. She was more focused on the wedding to-do list for her cousin's wedding. Now that they'd met Willow, Joan had forgiven the mix up about the town car and was excited to help. "Well, according to your itinerary," Sierra said, "you'll need energy to do everything you want, so you need your protein. And orange juice with champagne does not count." Sierra reached for her glass. "Although, it does taste delicious." She licked her lips and grinned at her friend. "Oh come on. Why so grumpy? Don't you like Willow?"

"Of course, I do." Joan sighed and shook her head. "I don't know what's wrong with me. Nothing tastes good today." She grimaced. "Not even the mimosas."
~~~

"No problem. I'm drinking yours so it doesn't go to waste."

Joan's cell phone buzzed again. Set on vibrate, the small smart phone danced across the table. Sierra watched Joan ignore it. "So," she asked, "what's going on with you and Max?"

Scowling, Joan grabbed her phone and dropped it into her purse. "We are at a tipping point, I'm afraid." She looked at her friend defiantly. "And no, I don't want to talk about it. Are you finished?"

"I am. Just take a couple more bites, and then we'll go."

"No need to talk to me like I'm a toddler." Joan pushed her chair back, tossing her napkin on her plate. "I'm done. Let's go meet Willow." And with that, she turned and walked out the restaurant, leaving Sierra to pay the bill.

"Okay, Ms. Grouchy Pants," Sierra flagged down their waitress. A minute later she found Joan waiting outside, waiting, her attention focused on the street.

"Well," Joan said slowly, checking her watch, "We're early. I think we should walk over to Robson St." She glanced up at Sierra. "This way, we don't miss a thing. Oh, and no going back and forth across the street. Got it?"

For just a moment Sierra's heart hurt as she thought her friend was referring to the mishap that happened while in Ireland in May. Visiting shops together while on the way to meet their guys at a pub, they'd become separated. Chaos had ensued, and Sierra felt blamed for being the one who 'wandered off'. It wasn't what happened, and it still irked her. The incident became moot considering how the rest of the trip went.

It made for some hurt feelings, mostly her own. She glanced down at her right hand. Okay, so the tip of her ring finger was gone, down to the first knuckle. It wasn't really *that* noticeable. A long scar now ran from the base of her palm, up to the newly healed incision. One of several, the dark, red scars covered the palm of her hand. Still tender to the touch, everything was healing now, including her heartache. And yet...

"Don't go there." She felt a tug on her shirtsleeve and caught Joan watching her. "I only meant," Joan continued, "this way, we don't miss any store we may want to check out later. Okay?" Sierra nodded.

"Good." Joan's stomach gave a loud rumble. "I want to find a pharmacy, or some kind of Walgreens type store. I think I need some Tums." She pulled out her phone and checked the map and turned to face the other way. "We'll go this way, over to Water Street and take a right. I believe there's a shopping center over there."

Joan found what she needed, and they made their way back to Robson Street. This time, they decided to take Abbott and head south. Stopping at the corner of Pender Street, they found themselves at the edge of Chinatown. "So, what do you think?" Sierra asked. "Do we have any time left to look around? Or should I grab us a cab?"

Joan opened her mouth to answer as loud drumming and the crashing of cymbals from behind jarred the air. "What the heck?" They both jumped back from the curb and edged up against an old building. Moments later a guy with a camera appeared, with an assistant that guided him as he walked backwards, his camera facing towards a dragon.

It's large head, the size of a small car, painted bright red and yellow, with ferocious black eyes glided left and right. The mouth, painted with blood red lips, stretched over large white fangs while it's long glittering serpent tongue dangled towards the street. The body made of shimmering iridescent fabric danced serpentine down the street. Its many legs covered in black jeans showing feet in different colored tennis shoes. Costumed drummers walked along side of the dragon, beating their drums.

"Wow, this is great." Sierra clapped her hands, grinning from ear to ear. This was the best show yet.

"I don't get it. It's not Chinese New Year," grumbled Joan, who covered her ears as the dragon paraded past them. Two young men with small video cameras followed, capturing crowd reaction.

Sierra turned to her friend and studied her pale, sad face. "You really don't feel good, do you?" Joan shook her head. "Okay. Then we're skipping the window shopping." Holding her hand up, she deflected Joan's disapproval. "I'm going to find you some Miso soup."

A few minutes later Sierra had Joan settled in a dark, red leather booth. The restaurant was quiet, a pleasant relief from the drums and cymbals. Sierra was searching the menu.

"And why do I want miso soup?" Joan asked, a little belligerent at finding herself no longer in charge of the situation.

"It's just like chicken noodle soup. Except that it has tofu and seaweed in it instead of chicken and noodles. It's served hot, and will help you feel better." Sierra kept a straight face, her eyes on her friend. "C'mon, give it a try. It can't hurt you; it can only make you feel better. Honest."

"I hate being treated like a baby." Joan wasn't about to give up being grumpy. "But I'll give it a try. It makes sense." She set down the menu. "And some hot tea, too." She grabbed her phone. "I'm texting Willow, letting her know we may be a little late."

"Good idea," Sierra said. The waitperson stepped up to their table. "Two bowls of miso soup, and hot tea, please." With a nod the young man picked up the menus and left.

"I feel like we're getting extra entertainment this week, for free." Sierra said, gazing out the window as a group of about twenty zombies lumbered by slowly on stiffened legs, passing the restaurant. "Wow. Those aren't even the same zombies from yesterday. With all these skits being filmed, I can't tell what's real from what's fake." Joan's raised eyebrows made Sierra rethink her statement. "Wait, I mean," she amended, "except for the zombies. You know what I mean." Their soup and tea arrived and both ladies leaned forward to smell the steam rising from the soup.

Joan watched Sierra take a careful sip from the small ceramic spoon. "You know, if you're hungry, you can order something else to eat."

"No, I'm fine. This is good, I like the sliced green onions floating on top."

Joan's phone buzzed. She took a quick glance and tossed it back into her purse. She made a show of picking up her teacup with both hands.

"Usually, you laugh off Max's bad jokes." Sierra watched her friend closely, and waited.

Joan was not going to cooperate. "Yes, I do, but not this time. And I told you, I don't want to talk about it."

"Fine." Sierra said airily. "How's the soup? Do you think the tea is calming down your stomach?"

"The soup tastes good, and the tea is going down. Let's leave it at that."

Sierra picked up her bowl and drank the rest of her soup.

Joan looked melancholy. "Do you think I'm ruining the weekend?"

"That depends. Are you upset about Willow?"

"What? Why would I be upset about Willow?"

Sierra shrugged. "Does the age difference with Willow being older than your cousin matter to you?"

"Are you kidding? So she's older than him. Good for her. It's only fourteen years. Men marry women younger than themselves all the time. She's friendly, has a fun sense of humor. I like how she's quick on the hugs. She's got to be in chronic pain, but you'd never know it. She teaches yoga, for heaven's sake. And stays active. And she's willing to move to the other side of the world? My cousin is a very lucky guy. Besides, I'd be a hypocrite to criticize her, since I'm ten years older than Max."

"Were all your men younger than you?"

"Just my boyfriends." She shrugged and spread her hands. "My first husband, Jake, and I were the same age. Husband number two, Frank, was two year older." Joan pushed aside her bowl of soup. "Some men, and Charles Henry is one of them, are older than their chronological age. He's always been more interested in what a woman thinks, rather than how she looks."

"So..." Sierra hesitated, wanting to word her next question carefully. "What category does Max fit in?"

"Good question." Joan watched the waiter bring over their bill. "We'll leave it up to the fortune cookies."

"So, what do you think of this 'Indie Video' contest?" Sierra asked him, as she handed him cash.

"It's crazy." He shook his head. "You saw the zombies, right?" They nodded. "If you think the zombies are weird, you should take a peek at what's going on in the alleys."

"The alleys?"

"Oh yeah, but police are starting to crack down and demand proof of permit."

"Proof of permit?" Now Joan was interested.

"Oh yeah, you have to have a permit to do any movie making. Even commercials. Doesn't matter. No matter how short. You get caught, it costs big bucks." He glanced at the cash. "Have a nice day ladies," he said, nodding his thanks. Sierra and Joan wrestled with the wrappers to get into their fortune cookies.

"Get ready for a new adventure," Sierra read. She frowned, glancing at her right hand. "Hmm, that makes me a little nervous. What does yours say?"

Joan stared at the small piece of paper for several moments before she spoke. "Someone new is coming into your life soon."

"Well, that would mean Willow, your cousin's soon to be wife. Or...maybe that means Max will be leaving your life?"

"Either that, or I'll never be rid of him." Joan stood up. "I'll meet you outside, I'm hitting the ladies room."

Sierra watched her walk away. They never talked about the money, but it had to be strange, and more than a little worrisome, never really knowing for sure if the person you loved, loved you. Or your money. Grabbing her purse, she waved at the waiter as she left.

It was several minutes later when Joan came out of the restaurant. Sierra watched her, a goofy smirk on her face. "So," she asked her. "Was it shock, or surprise?"

Joan shot her a look. "Okay, so you were flashed by the university nympho babes too?"

"Oh yeah, they ran up to me and the darker blonde pulled up her top as another gal snapped my picture. Turns out they're creating a video collage of all the different responses."

They started looking for a taxi. "You have to admit," Sierra continued, "it's a cute idea." Joan just smiled. "No, really, I think that's great creativity. And very different. You have to admit it's a better idea than the stupid jousting match we saw yesterday in the park. Unless of course, someone caught you on video losing control of your bike and falling into the pond." Joan still ignored her. "I figured," Sierra said, trying again, "the college girls will fit in the 'shock' category. What do you think?"

"You sent those gals into the restroom." It was a statement, not a question. "You're not going to let this go, are you?"

"What happened?" Sierra couldn't stop grinning.

"I got an eyeful. Then I pointed out how her left boob was droopier than the right. And I walked away. In fact, I think I left them...in shock." She was grinning now, too.

"You are so bad!" Sierra grabbed Joan's arm as they laughed.

"That's why we're friends." Joan pulled out her notepad. "This is Friday, right?" she asked.

"Yep, all day. Why?"

"Just checking the schedule. We've got the rest of today to finalize everything with Willow here in Vancouver, then tomorrow morning we check out and catch the Sea to Sky train to Whistler."

Sierra smiled. "I haven't been on a train ride in years. Have you been on it before?"

Joan nodded.

"With which husband?" Sierra asked, half teasing.

"Neither. Our family used to vacation up at Whistler for a couple of months each summer when I was in high school."

"Nice. Hotel or condo?" Sierra grabbed Joan's shoulder to keep her from stepping off the sidewalk corner. The light had turned red.

"A condo," Joan said. "My folks liked the privacy. And in the long run, it was better renting than staying at the lodge."

"What did you like about the summers up there?" Sierra watched her friend's face turn pink. "What?" she demanded. "Tell me."

"It was the 80's, what do you expect?" Joan's grin deepened. "Hot summer, hot boys, hot music, hot ..." She trailed off and released a deep sigh. "Wow, I haven't thought of those years in a long time."

The light turned green, and they stepped forward in unison, crossing the street and watching a group of bicyclists glide downhill past them.

"Hey," Sierra pointed at the group. "Do you want to--"

"No." Joan's reply sharp, and to the point.

Passing an alley, Sierra couldn't resist looking. Sure enough, there were a group of people standing around a couple of old lawn chairs and what looked like a small wooden table. An old, beat up, Igloo cooler sat on the hot cement nearby. One of the men appeared dressed as a police officer. Another guy was holding a camera, two other guys stood apart from the group, and a young woman stood near the cameraman with a dog held tightly close to her with a leash. Sierra stopped suddenly, frozen.

The tourists walking behind her weren't happy; glaring, they huffed at her as they walked around her. "What do you see?" Joan asked. She saw people, but couldn't figure out what caught Sierra's attention.

"That woman is holding a blue Great Dane puppy. He can't be more than four months old."

"You're blocking traffic. To look at a dog?"

"Well, apparently they're getting ready to shoot their video. I want to see how they use the dog." Sierra took a couple of tentative steps towards them. They were easily a half block away. She couldn't hear the dialog, but the body language spoke volumes, the woman and dog was being attacked. The dog started yelping, and whimpering in pain. Now Sierra began running. She didn't know, or care, if this was part of the act. No way would she let anyone, for any reason, hurt a dog.

Sierra could hear Joan following her, but the dog's scared cries made her run faster. Passing a dumpster she grabbed a short piece of two by four leaning against it, and kept on going. The guy dressed as the policeman was kicking at the dog and tugging at its collar, while the woman encouraged the dog to attack him. The cameraman was facing them. No one saw Sierra coming up.

She yelled as she slammed the 2x4 across the policeman's shoulders. Again, and again. "You bastard! Stop hurting that dog. Stop it. Stop it." The woman froze and the policeman dropped to his knees. The cameraman did a full 360 turn before stopping the camera on Sierra.

"How dare you!" Sierra shouted at them. "How dare you abuse this helpless animal, are you crazy?" She got in two more hits before she rounded on the others standing nearby, the piece of wood still in her hand like a baseball bat. "How can you do this? What's the matter with you?" Angry and in tears, she dropped to her knees to hug the shivering puppy, the piece of wood still in her hand.

Joan finally caught up with her, holding up her cell phone. "I've called 911, don't you dare try anything."

The woman whirled around, holding an empty blue cloth bag. She stepped back, cradling the bag in her arms. "Who are you?" she demanded. "We're in the middle of a shoot."

"You crazy bitch, what's the matter with you?" The man who Sierra had targeted was still on the ground, holding his left arm close to his chest.

"You've ruined everything." Near tears, the young woman's legs sagged as she dropped into a lawn chair next to the cooler. She started blowing out short, hard breaths and rubbing her abdomen. It quickly became apparent that this woman was very pregnant.

Sierra and Joan exchanged glances. What *was* going on? Keeping a tight grip on the dog's collar, Sierra turned to the man she'd seen standing across the alley. "What did you see?" But the alley behind her was empty. "Where'd he go?"

"There's only the three of us," the would-be policeman replied sullenly. He slowly got to his feet. "Just us," he said again. "And the mutt."

"Hey!" Joan was kneeling by the panting woman. "I think we need to call an ambulance."

"No, no." The young woman struggled onto her feet. The lawn chair had seen better days, the cheap plastic woven straps faded and frayed. The flimsy metal frame was dented, appearing ready to collapse at any moment.

The dog whined, and broke free from Sierra's grasp. He stumbled over to the woman, every inch of his sleek gray body shivering. Standing as close as he could to her, he leaned against her knees, his tail whipping anyone within range. Including Joan, who caught the tip of the tail on her arm. "Ow, that's going to leave a bruise," she mumbled under her breath.

"Oh, sweet baby, it's okay." Sierra leaned over to rub the dog's ears, trying to calm him and determine any damage. She could see several welts on the dog's back and ribs.

Rising quickly, it took her just two steps, for her nose was an inch from the dog abuser. "You should be arrested." She spat the words from clenched lips. "Or perhaps, you need a beating of your own."

"Trust me, you stupid cow, I already got it. I didn't hit the dog that hard. I just wanted to make him whine and cry in fear." It took him a couple of moments before he realized how bad that sounded. Sierra, if anything, moved closer. Her narrowed eyes mere slits, signaling further danger.

"I'm, I mean...it's in the script." He pointed frantically at the cameraman and the woman, who was now petting the dog. He drew a breath and tried again. "We're making a video, okay? You know? We're entering it in the Indie Video competition. To win a million dollars, you know?"

"You've ruined everything."

Sierra and Joan stared at the woman. Her hair was dark brown, with blonde streaks all throughout except for her bangs. They were stark red.

"So," Joan asked, motioning toward the red bangs. "What's with the hair? Are you supposed to be Scary Spice or Surprise Spice?"

"What?" the woman's hand flew to her hair.

"You know, the Spice Girls? They were a girl band...never mind." She was still rubbing her arm. "That dog's tail should be registered as a lethal weapon."

"Tell me about it," the cameraman muttered. He'd finally turned off the camera and held it carefully with both hands. "No worries guys. I think I've got some great stuff here. We're good." He looked over at the girl. "Honey, if they called the cops we have to leave." He turned back to Joan. "Since we don't have a permit and you've ratted us out, we need to find another place to finish the scene."

Sierra took a closer look at the woman. She appeared five, maybe seven, years younger than her, but she looked tired, with dark circles under her eyes and weariness in her stance. Sierra looked over at Joan, her mouth open to mention this fact, and was surprised to see Joan looking just as weary, if not a little greener. "Joan, are you okay?" Before her friend could answer she turned away and vomited. Unfortunately, for the cameraman, Joan grabbed his camera bag.

"Apparently, the miso soup helped," Sierra said, as she pulled a couple of tissues out of her pocket for Joan.

"Seriously?" The faux policeman wasn't amused. "What the hell? That was brand new."

Chapter THREE

"I can't believe the taxi driver let us bring the dog." Joan whispered to Sierra. Despite Joan's protests and misgivings, the dog snuggled quietly between the two women in the back seat, his large head and one paw resting in Sierra's lap.

Sierra kept her 'I told you so' to herself as the taxi turned off the busy street and into a residential neighborhood. Both women were busy with their own thoughts. Joan, looking over her copy of Willow's notes, and Sierra, thinking ahead on how to deal with authorities, and Marcus, so she could get her new dog into the States.

That incident in the alley. What a crazy situation. She gently rubbed the puppy's muzzle, not minding the long, wet tongue licking her fingers. After Joan had been sick, everybody scattered, leaving Sierra and Joan to face the police alone. Sierra had never seen anybody disappear so fast like the threesome in the alley, except maybe the guy who apparently disappeared as she run past him. She was sure she'd seen someone standing there, watching that group filming.

Police arrived shortly thereafter, finding only Sierra, Joan, and the Great Dane puppy. Also left behind were the broken down lawn chairs, the old Igloo cooler with four bottled waters, and the wooden table. The officers could do nothing so they left...without the dog.

Sierra observed the houses as they drove by, flexing her left hand. She could feel a few splinters caught under the skin, especially in the fleshy area between her thumb and forefinger. That had been a foolish and thoughtless move. The faux policeman could have easily had a weapon of his own. Or he could have decided to fight back. Or he could have decided to have her arrested for assault. And since it had been recorded, perhaps he still could. Her fingers curled, gently filled with soft, loose, puppy fur and long, soft, silky puppy ears.

Hearing the dog's cries had caused Sierra to see red. Literally. So angry, so focused on reacting, it was as if her eyes were filmed over with blood. Sighing, she leaned down and kissed the puppy's nose. She glanced over at Joan. Would her friend complain to Marcus? Or in Joan's eye, did she look brave, albeit, foolhardy?

The taxi turned and pulled over to the shaded sidewalk. "Wow," Joan said. "Nice house." The taxi had pulled up in front of a large, two story, detached house with a covered front porch. A large metal square sign, with several balloons attached, its legs firmly planted into the thick green grass, advertised an Estate Sale in Progress. 9:00am till 4:00pm, and by appointment.

Sierra barely got one leg out of the cab before the puppy jumped over her, and onto the grass, dragging the leash behind him. "At least they left the dog's leash," she said. He ambled over to the sign and peed. "Good boy," Sierra said. She beamed at Joan. "See? He's going to be fine." She turned her attention to the property. "I like how the lawn slopes up to the steps," Sierra said. "It gives the house a 'castle on the hill' look. Don't you think?"

Joan gave the house an appraising look, taking in the tall cypress trees standing sentry at each corner of the yard. The trees towered over the two-story house, giving the property a Mediterranean feel. She liked it. Glancing over at Sierra she did a double take. "You're not taking the dog with you into the house," Joan spoke firmly, clearly making a statement, not a question.

"Absolutely I am," Sierra retorted. "If Willow disapproves, I'll take him out back and find some shade for him." She bent down and rubbed the dog's head. "Willow strikes me as an animal lover. I wouldn't be surprised if she has five cats."

Joan closed her eyes. "Lord, have mercy," she whispered. Opening her eyes again, she faced Sierra. "She's having an Estate Sale. Everything has to be pristine." Joan shook her head. "There's bound to be breakables, and that dog's tail reminds me of a wrecking ball. He'll break something." Two cars parked across the street, and several people were walking towards the house.

"I'll watch him." Sierra replied. "If he breaks something, then I'll buy it." She threw Joan a look. "I guess I'll have to make sure it's not an *antique*."

Joan pulled open the storm door. The porch was clean, and the railing freshly painted. The love seat sat to the left of the door, a simple piece covered in off white canvas fabric, looked inviting. Perfect place to relax and read the morning paper in the summer. But then, the natural stained maple rocker in the other corner looked comfy, too. Both were accented with blue and white throw pillows.

The front door was a heavy, oversized wood door painted in red. A large, brass doorknocker shaped like a monkey's head hung in the top middle of the door, forever grinning. Sierra stepped up behind Joan and lifted the brass monkey's knocker nose and tapped lightly. A price sticker showed from the lower lip of the monkey head.

"You know," Sierra said. "This is cute - and different. I think I'll buy this."

Joan rolled her eyes. "Seriously?" She grabbed the doorknob and pushed the door open. "Hey, Willow, we're here."

Sierra and Joan found themselves standing in the foyer that opened into the living room. Hickory floors, high ceilings with skylights made the space feel open and welcoming. The warm, cream-colored walls were perfect. Joan turned away from the living room and followed the hardwood into a formal dining room.

Long and rectangular, the polished wood dining table and eight matching chairs sat ready with a full service for eight already set out, complete with a full service of china and silverware. Each place setting also had one crystal wine stem.

"This makes for a heck of a party," Sierra said. "This should be photographed for a magazine spread in Home Beautiful, or something." The Dane puppy wagged its tail in agreement, banging against one of the chair legs.

"It would look beautiful in your home, I'm sure." A prim, frosty voice replied. Sierra and Joan looked up towards the kitchen entryway. There they saw a woman in a crisp, two piece navy blue suit. A clipboard in one hand a pager in the other. She smiled without wrinkling her eyes. "Good afternoon, ladies. My name is Gwendolyn Matthew-Symms. I'm the estate manager." She pointed at the table. "You have great taste. This table is hard maple, as you can see, it seats eight. There is a table extension available that will extend it to seat a dinner party for twelve, if necessary." She turned and pointed towards the china hutch, next to Joan. "There are four sets of china to choose from. In addition, there are lots of platters and serving pieces to choose from as well. If you're looking for silver, I have..."

Gwendolyn Matthew-Symms froze, stopping in mid-sentence. Sierra and Joan looked at each other. Uh oh. "What. Is. That." Gwendolyn pointed the pager down at Sierra's legs.

"Well," Sierra started. "In general, it's a dog. Specifically, he is a blue Great Dane puppy. Probably around four months old."

The estate manager started making little squeaking noises. Sierra watched the woman swallow hard. "Your dog is sitting on an original Turkish hand knotted, silk on wool rug." She squeezed the pager in her hand, pressing a button over and over. "Bernice? Bernice? I need you in the dining room. Now. Code red, repeat. Code red."

Joan raised her eyebrows. "There's no need to be upset. The dog is perfectly house trained." Sierra nodded. A complete lie, of course. Or, maybe it could be true.

A woman, also with a clipboard, pager and a roll of paper towels walked up behind Gwendolyn. She was taller than the estate manager, with an easy smile and friendly eyes. "What's up, Gwen?"

The blond could only point. So Sierra stepped forward, gently tugging on the leash. The puppy, however, was now sound asleep on the carpet under one of the chairs. "I think she's freaked out over the dog," Sierra said.

"Oh, let's see." Bernice, dressed in dark slacks, light blue collared shirt and dark blue apron with the Royal Estates logo, knelt down and peered under the table. "It's a Dane puppy. Oh, he is adorable." She gently pulled him into her arms. "How about I take him out back? There's shade and water, and a little fenced area. He won't get out. You ladies can browse as long as you like."

"That's fine," Sierra said, watching Gwendolyn. The estate manager was backing away from the dog as if it were a wild animal.

"Well, now," Gwendolyn said, "I'm sure your dog is just wonderful, but I'm responsible for all the estate items."

"We understand," Joan said. "Actually, we're here to see Ms. Jackson."

"Oh." A funny look crossed her face. "Was she...expecting you?"

"Yes, she is." Joan smiled thinly. "We're here to finalize her wedding preparations. You know she's getting married tomorrow, right? Is she in her yoga studio?"

Gwendolyn stepped back "I...I only just heard last night that she was getting married. I knew she was moving, of course." She gave a little laugh as she motioned to the kitchen table. "Who's she getting married to, exactly?" Her eyes glittered and her lips lifted in a half-hearted attempt at a smile.

Joan and Sierra exchanged a look. They weren't feeling a happy vibe from this woman. "Willow is marrying my cousin, Charles Henry Bishop."

"Oh. Ah, well, I know Charles Henry. He's quite the catch. Lucky Willow." Gwendolyn turned her face away from Joan and Sierra, pretending to rearrange a set of wine glasses. She cleared her throat. "He's your cousin?"

Joan nodded.

"Hmm," Gwendolyn slowly shook her head. "That's too bad."

"What?" Joan asked. "Why do you say that?"

"Well, actually, the bride to be..." she cleared her throat. "The bride to be has had an accident."

"What kind of accident? Is Willow okay?" Joan's voice turned sharp, drawing herself up to her full five foot four inches.

"Not exactly." Gwendolyn's hands were flexing, her breath short. "Apparently Ms. Jackson fell down the stairs."

"What? When was this?"

"She was found early this morning, crumpled in a heap at the bottom of the stairs. A couple of her 6:00am yoga students found her, and called the police and ambulance. But it was...too late. It appears she died from breaking her neck."

"But we were with her, just last night," Sierra said. She turned toward her friend. "Joan, I'm so sorry-" Joan held her hand up sharply. Sierra stopped talking, frozen to her spot.

Arms crossed now, Joan leaned heavily against the china hutch, her eyes narrowed and her lips pursed. She ignored the china pieces being shoved against each other by her hips.

Gwendolyn grimaced, pulling firmly on Joan's shoulder. "Why don't we sit in the living room, shall we?" Joan allowed herself to be guided over to the next room and sat on one side of the cream colored couch. Sierra quickly sat down next to her.

"Tell me what happened, Gwendolyn," Joan's voice cracked. Her hands clasped together in a tight ball.

"It's Ms. Matthew-Symms," Gwendolyn corrected. "All I know is Ms. Jackson hired me as her estate manager to sell her personal property as quickly as possible. Her plans were to use the funds to move to Australia."

"Did you know Ms. Jackson before she hired you?"

"What are you implying?" Gwendolyn's eyes flared wide. "I have been handling estate sales in the entire British Columbia area for over nine years now."

"I'm sure you have," Joan said. "My cousin would only have hired the best."

"Oh." The estate manager appeared suddenly speechless.

"How long have you been working on Willow's estate" Sierra asked, nudging Joan's leg.

The woman checked her clipboard. "I was hired on the first of this month, so, three weeks."

"Did you ever meet any of her yoga clients?" Sierra asked softly.

"Well, yes," admitted Gwendolyn. "Several of them, actually. I used to attend her classes." She pulled at her skirt and straightened her papers before looking up at Joan.

"This is...a shock," Joan said coolly, meeting her gaze.

"I know," Gwendolyn agreed, eyes wide. "Imagine how I felt, coming here this morning finding police cars in the driveway."

"Do the police think it's a break-in? Sierra asked.

"No sign of a break-in. Nothing appears to be missing. I gave the police the inventory I have on all her items. I believe there was a question about her medication. Had she been drinking last night?"

Sierra and Joan looked at each other. The champagne. Was this their fault?

"Yet, you're going ahead with the estate sale," Joan said softly, ignoring Gwendolyn's question. She watched a couple of ladies walk in from the kitchen and into the dining room.

Gwendolyn nodded sadly and shrugged. "I talked to her mother. After the police notified her, of course," she added quickly, seeing the look on Joan's face. "She said to go ahead. The family had already had the chance to pick out what they wanted. And all her other personal things are already stored in a POD, by the yoga studio."

"All her things?" Joan asked sharply.

"Except for what she had packed in her bedroom. Yes. She was scheduled to leave the country on Tuesday."

"After the wedding," Joan said softly, more to herself than Gwendolyn.

"After what?" Gwendolyn asked.

"After the wedding." Sierra spoke up, as Joan merely swallowed hard and looked away. "Willow and Charles Henry? They were to be married Saturday. At Whistler."

"Charles Henry..." Gwendolyn closed her eyes her gloved hands balled into fists.

"My cousin." Joan said, her voice stronger now. "Charles Henry is my cousin." She glanced over at Sierra. "He's still in Australia. I need to call him."

"The police reached Willow's mother with her cell phone." Gwendolyn turned and face Joan. "They assured her it was an accident." She looked past Joan and Sierra as more clients walked into the house. "Excuse me," she said. She stood, smoothing the invisible wrinkles from her skirt. A big smile now plastered on her face, Gwendolyn moved toward the women and introduced herself. She handed them each a flyer.

Sierra and Joan watched her walk away. "Well," Joan said, "we've been dismissed. What do we do now?"

Sierra stood up, grabbing her friend with her. "As soon as she shows those ladies into the den - we make a dash for the stairs."

"The stairs?" A flash of pain crossed Joan's face.

"C'mon." Sierra pulled her up the stairs. "Grab the handrail, we're checking Willow's room."

"Should we even be walking on these stairs?" Joan asked. "What if we're walking on something important?" Joan was staring down at the marble tile at the bottom of the stairs.

"Joan, the police said it was an accident, that's all. A horrible, sad mistake."

The room was easy to find, it was the only one with a bed. And two pieces of luggage, already packed, standing guard by the door. The connecting bathroom was stripped down to bare essentials. Sierra noticed all the toiletries were travel size, from previous hotel stays. A couple of paperback books were stacked on the only end table, along with the same shabby-chic hobo bag Willow carried the night before. A half dozen bottles of medication and supplements crowded around a small clock-radio.

A quilt lay across Willow's queen size bed, smooth, flat, with no creases. Did she die before she'd gone to bed last night? Or had the bed been made up, to look that way? Joan stared down at the quilt, then reached for a corner and flipped it back. There was a stitched tag, listing the date and name of the quilter. "My aunt made this," Joan said. "Charles Henry's mother. She made one for me, too. He liked the natural tones of earth and sky."

"I bet I can guess what colors your quilt is made with," Sierra said.

"You think so?"

"Absolutely. It's all jewel tones. Right?"

Joan offered a small smile at that, and nodded. "Okay, smartass, you're right."

Sierra opened another slider door. "Hey, she has a walk in closet. This is cool." A large rectangular room, it was easily seven foot by ten foot, with built in shelves that went all the way around. There was a small pile of empty shoeboxes and tissue paper stacked against the back wall. A long, lonely shoe rack sat on the floor along a wall. The only pair of shoes left in the closet were a pair of well used, comfy looking, dingy yellow, wooly slippers. Hanger bars were positioned under the shelves. They, too, snaked around the room. And like the shelves, virtually empty. Huddled together in a small space right next to the door, hung a half dozen leotards and yoga pants.

"Looks like she was down to just the essentials for the last several days," Sierra said.

"I wonder why she didn't keep her wedding dress here." Joan asked. "I mean, I know she wasn't wearing a gown, but still, there's plenty of room to store it."

"Maybe she was worried her dress would get mixed in with the estate sale items." Sierra fingered the folds of fabric of the yoga pants while admiring the colors. "They look comfortable." She felt something firm. She lifted a hanger and carried it over to the bed. "There's something hidden here."

Joan sat next to her. "What are you doing?"

"Just a minute." Sierra, fumbling with several layers of pants pulled out a small journal. Nothing fancy, the cardboard covers were creased and the paper well worn. "It's a journal, of sorts," Sierra said.

"Let me see," Joan snatched it from her friend's hands. She stood up and started walking around the room.

Normally, Sierra would have been sticking her face in the journal as well. But recognizing Joan's feelings for her cousin's loss, she held her tongue and waited. And watched.

Joan appeared mesmerized, walking back and forth in front of the bed, reading from one page to the next. Sierra watched as she turned and sat down at the foot of the bed, her nose still in the book.

"Hey," Sierra said. "Do you know your lips move when you read?"

Joan merely held up her hand, a moment later she looked up. "What? I do not," she blustered. "This is amazing," she continued. "It's a jewelry journal."

"It's a...what?" Sierra was sure she hadn't heard correctly.

"This is awesome. Willow has written all about the pieces of jewelry her husband gave her. Each one has a story." Joan looked up at Sierra. "This should be mandatory for all men. Her first husband was a real Mr. Romance."

"Do you think Charles Henry is in it?"

"Hmmm." Joan flipped to the back of the journal. Then she smiled. "Yes, he's in it. Listen to this... in February she met Charles Henry, and here she's added the details of how CH gave her the earrings, and asked her to marry him in August. There's even a picture of the earrings, with all the info on carat weight and value of stones. Whoa, they're set in platinum, not white gold. Cha-ching."

Suddenly, Joan closed the journal, holding it tightly in her hands. "Where are the earrings? Willow was wearing them last night. Why didn't this Ms. Matthew-Symms say anything about the wedding? Or, at least, that Willow was getting married?"

"Did she know? She sounded a little shocked when we asked her about it. And besides," Sierra continued, "Willow said she was keeping everything low key."

"True," Joan's gaze turned hard. "And, she said she'd told her estate sales manager earlier this week. That's the Ms. Matthew-Symms. So wouldn't *she* know about the wedding? And the earrings Willow's been wearing for, what, almost two months?"

"But, why should she care?" Sierra asked.

Joan took a sudden breath. "Wait, Willow said she met Charles Henry when he attended one of her yoga classes. He came as a guest. But whose guest?"

They looked at each other. "Something's...not right," Sierra said.

Joan nodded. "And I'm going to find out what."

Sierra shook her head. "You mean, *we're* going to find out."

"For Charles Henry," Joan said, getting to her feet.

Sierra nodded. "We've got appointments to keep." They closed the bedroom door behind them. Joan led the way to the stairs, but Sierra stopped her. The stairs were light oak hardwood, with a glossy finish. So much more than just functional, the stairs made a statement. With the top of the landing where Sierra and Joan stood, being seven feet wide and sweeping down and open into the main entry of the home.

The bottom of the landing was ten feet wide. To Sierra, it looked like something out of *Gone with the Wind.* She wished she had a staircase just like it. "Step slowly," she told Joan. "Perhaps, if the police believe her death was an accident, they might have missed something. You never know." Sierra grabbed the polished wood rail on one side as Joan reached for the other.

"What are we looking for?" Joan whispered. At the moment they were alone, but she could hear other people's conversations throughout the house.

"I don't know," Sierra shrugged. "But if something is here, it'll probably be on one of the lower steps." She swallowed hard, realizing it had been Willow's last step in life.

Taking their time, they moved cautiously, as if stepping on eggshells. The glossy finish of the stairs was spotless. The marble tile floor at the landing showed some scuffmarks. But that could have been from the EMT's, or an earlier bargain hunter. They both stood at the bottom of the stairs, looking up. Nothing. No torn fabric, no buttons, no broken railing. No proof. It was impossible to tell that anything tragic had happened.

Joan was angry, blinking rapidly to keep the tears away. Her thoughts crowded her mind. Were they just supposed to accept this, and move on? Oh well, Willow fell down the stairs - and died - the day before she was going to be married? Oh, and by the way, her engagement earrings are missing. No big deal. Just a mega - expensive gift from her soon to be husband, nothing sinister here. Move along. Charles Henry was going to be devastated. "Let's pick up Willow's personal effects," Joan said.

"Just give me one more minute..." Sierra squatted at the base of the stairs, her feet flat on the floor.

"How can you do that? Joan asked. "You make my knees hurt just watching you."

Sierra bent lower to look under the tread lip of the last step. "I see a smudge of red here. Not sure what-"

"Ladies!"

Joan whirled around, bumping into Sierra, causing her to fall back onto the floor slamming an elbow against the bottom step. Sierra grumbled as she pushed against the lower stair to sit up, while rubbing her elbow. "Hey, what's your problem?"

Gwendolyn, clipboard held tight against her chest glared at Joan and Sierra. "You two must leave. Now. I've got clients interested in the living room furniture. I don't need you two creating a spectacle." She looked down at Sierra. "What happened to your finger?" She pointed at Sierra's injured hand. Sierra pulled her hand back, and quickly shoved her fist into her sweater pocket.

"Wow, I don't think *that's* going to grow back," the estate manager said smugly. "I'm always careful with my hands." She waved her white-gloved hands briefly in front of Sierra and Joan. "I don't dare wash dishes or clean. All that dust and chemicals. It ruins your skin. My grandmother lost two fingers. Got them caught in the washing machine. Disfigured her for life."

Sierra tugged at Joan. "Let's go. I want to get the dog."

Joan sputtered as she let Sierra pull her through the kitchen and out the back door. "I have *never* heard such rudeness. When I talk to Charles Henry...her ass is fired." She continued grumbling, following Sierra on the graveled path that led to the yoga studio. There, in a shady spot of thick, green grass was the Dane puppy. Sleeping.

Bernice stepped out of the yoga studio. "You're leaving already?"

Joan glared at her. "How can you stand to work with that woman?"

"She can be difficult." Bernice wiped her hands on her apron, then handed the dog leash to Sierra. "I should know, she's my sister. Basically, I stay out of her way and let Rupert deal with her." A sardonic smile crossed her face. "He's our older brother. The money is good, and usually I don't deal too much with her - she hates to get her hands dirty."

"So she said," Joan replied coldly.

"For what it's worth, I think Willow's death rattled her. It's rattled all of us." She reached out and rubbed the now wide-awake puppy's silky ears. "I still can't believe it. I mean, yesterday was just a regular day. And now..."

"Did Willow seem ill? Or having any difficulties?"

"No. I know her rheumatoid arthritis had been acting up, but she didn't let that slow her down. I noticed she seemed pretty nervous the last couple of days." She looked at Joan. "Maybe she was worried about meeting you?"

"You do know Willow planned on getting married tomorrow?" Sierra asked.

Bernice's eyes widened. "Really? Wow. I thought she was excited about moving to Australia, but...wow." Her face darkened as she realized the significance. "Oh no, what about her fiancé? Does he know yet? Do you know who he is?"

"Charles Henry Bishop. My cousin," Joan said. "He's on his way back from Australia now."

"Who found her, do you know?" Sierra asked.

"Several of her clients," Bernice said. "She has...had a six AM yoga class this morning. Crazy, right? Anyway, her ladies were worried when the yoga room wasn't unlocked, or the lights on, so they came up to the house. One of them knew where the spare key is kept, and they let themselves in. They found Willow at the bottom of the stairs. One of them called the police. They were still here giving statements to the police when I arrived at eight." She caught Joan's look. "I didn't see the body, they had already moved Willow."

"Did you arrive first?" Sierra focused on stroking the dog's soft fur.

"I always do." Bernice rolled her eyes. "But not today. Gwendolyn and Rupert arrived before me. They're usually later. But then, it is the first day of the estate sale."

"About that," Joan said. "Doesn't that strike you as rather, distasteful?"

"Not really. Gwendolyn called Willow's mother after the police did, and she said to go ahead, it was what her daughter wanted." She shrugged. "Wow, Charles Henry and Willow, I had no idea. That won't go over well with--"

"Bernice!"

The ladies jumped at the voice, coming from a pager at Bernice's waist. "Go ahead," Bernice responded. She rubbed the Dane's head and gave Sierra and Joan a small wave as she started walking quickly back toward the house.

"What did she mean, this wedding wouldn't go over well? With who?" Joan asked.

Sierra shrugged. The puppy zigzagged ahead of her, straining on the leash. "So what happens now?" Sierra asked.

"First, a taxi. We're going back to the hotel." Joan looked over at the puppy. "Hopefully the concierge can find us a dog sitter." She raised her eyebrows at Sierra. "Are you sure I can't convince you to drop him off at the pound?" The mutinous look on her friend's face answered that.

Chapter FOUR

The only pleasant part of the afternoon was finding out the doorman would be happy to take care of the Dane puppy. Sierra was adamant that he understood he was merely dog sitting, she had every intention of taking the dog back to the States with her - no matter what Marcus would think or say about it.

Thankfully, the afternoon went faster than expected. It was hard to be the bearer of sad news to all the vendors involved in the wedding plans. Everywhere they went, they had to repeat the same gruesome news over and over. Everyone wanted details, but they didn't have any to offer.

At the bakery, after explaining what had happened, the owner brought out the cake for Joan and Sierra to see. It was breathtaking. Victorian style with three tiers, each tier wrapped in real lace, with butter cream iced edges and garnished white roses. The topper was a small bouquet of white roses with lace. With tears in her eyes, Joan took a picture of it with her cell phone and then asked the owner to donate the cake to another bride.

It wasn't any easier at the florist. Joan paid the balance due and told them the flowers would be used at Willow's funeral. She figured Charles Henry would determine when that would be. Or, would it be Willow's mother? They decided Willow should like to be buried with her bouquet of peonies and white roses.

The dress shop had been the hardest stop of all. Willow's dress of white satin covered in simple cream lace, dripping with white pearls was nothing short of divine. Joan thought if she ever got married again, she'd have a dress like this one. Joan decided it was the dress Willow should be buried in. Sierra reminded her again of Willow's mother in Victoria. Joan shrugged. It didn't matter. She'd let Charles Henry worry about that. They left the dress at the shop, saying someone would call back in a few days.

"How's your stomach doing?" Sierra asked as they left the dress shop. It was after 5 pm in the afternoon, and she was ready to sit down somewhere. Preferably somewhere with food and alcohol. They were both dragging.

"I don't know how I feel. I'm too numb," Joan said. Moving as one, they soon found themselves standing at the corner of Burrard and Alberni. Once again, less than 24 hours since they'd first met Willow, they found themselves back in the Golden Triangle. Sierra and Joan had become adept at dodging people with video cameras filming silly stunts. They were immune; none of it was exciting anymore. They'd had more than their share of surprise and shock.

"Well?" Sierra asked. "Are you up for one last stop?" It was a moot point. Of course they were going in to Tiffany's. The same doorman from the night before greeted them. "Welcome, ladies," he said, as he held open the door and motioned them inside.

They settled onto the same comfy, overstuffed chairs. Kris Query brought them each a bottled water. "You two look like you've been on your feet all day."

"Pretty much," Sierra said, savoring the fresh, cool water. "But this morning we were knocked off our feet."

"We've learned Willow is dead," Joan's voice sounded flat and tired.

"What?" Stunned, Kris turned away, blinking back tears. "When?"

"Good question. We don't know any details, yet. But it looks like either late last night, or very early this morning."

"What - What happened?"

"She was found dead at the bottom of her stairs, we're told she was still in her clothes from last night."

"Oh no, this is awful." Kris sat down next to them. "Was she in her pj's? Did she trip in those slippers? Can't they tell when she died?" She dabbed at her eyes with a tissue. "Does Charles Henry know? I'm sorry, Willow had become a friend to me, so much more than just a client."

"Those are some great questions," Sierra said. "We'd like answers too."

"Charles Henry is still in transit," Joan answered. "I've tried several times, but his phone goes straight to voicemail."

"What about Judith, Willow's mother?"

"The police called her-"

"Ah, wait," Sierra corrected, wagging a finger. "We were told by a third party, that the authorities contacted Willow's mother."

Joan frowned. "Why do you say it like that?"

"Because we haven't talked to the police. We've just taken the word of that snotty estate sales manager."

Kris sat up. "Estate manager? Are you talking about Ms. Matthew - Symms? Of Royal Estate Planning?"

Sierra and Joan nodded.

A sharp intake of breath followed a look of disdain flitting across Kris's face.

"You know her?" Sierra said.

"Oh yes, Miss Vancouver Island, and first runner-up in the Miss Canada pageant, at least ten years ago, probably more like thirteen. But she walks around like it was just last year."

"Perfect size four, every blonde hair in place, manicured nails," Sierra ticked off a complete description. "No wrinkles anywhere, perfect clothes, perfect shoes..."

"Enough already, you're making me nauseous." Joan gently rubbed her forehead.

"Well, maybe you're hungry. You did throw up lunch," Sierra said.

"Maybe you're in shock," Kris said, patting Joan's arm.

"No, she was already feeling puny," Sierra shared.

"Hello, I'm right here. Don't talk about me as if I'm a patient."

"How about some tea? I've got something soothing." Kris stood up. "Give me two minutes, I'll be right back."

Joan sighed as she watched the store manager walk away. "I'm tired, I'm upset, and I'm ready to go back to the hotel. Now."

Sierra nodded. "I understand. Hang in there, just one more thing, then we'll leave."

Joan looked at her suspiciously. "What 'one more thing'?"

"Shhh," Sierra looked up at Kris and smiled, reaching for her cup of tea. "Thank you, this is perfect."

The store manager set down a small plate of shortbread cookies, baked in intricate shapes of the maple leaf, Canada's national symbol. Watching Sierra and Joan drink their tea, Kris hesitated a moment. Then took the plunge. "I'm sorry, I have to ask. Where are the earrings? Are they with Willow's personal effects?"

"Good question," Joan said. She glanced at Sierra. "We haven't been told. We presumed she was wearing them since she had them on when she left here. But nobody's mentioned them."

Kris's eyebrows shot up at this. "They're missing?" She clamped her mouth shut.

"We're not sure at this time, but it's looking that way," Joan said, as she graced Sierra with a hard look.

"Say, Kris?" Sierra set down her tea cup and pulled a scrap of tissue from her jean's pocket. "Can you tell me if this is made of white gold, or platinum?" Sitting in her palm was a small looped piece of metal, resembling a half pretzel, with a short, sharp stub sticking out at the narrow end.

Kris carefully picked it up, and studied it closely. "It's our design. It appears to be the back of an earring. Definitely platinum, you can see it's been pulled away from the earring-"

She froze, her eyes meeting Sierra's. "This looks like a back of Willow's earrings. Where did you find it?"

"That's what I want to know." Joan sounded irritated. "Where did you find this? And when?"

"I found it at the bottom of the stairs this morning. Remember when you knocked me over? My hand was shoved underneath the lower stair, and I felt it there, pushed up against the wood."

"Oh, my God," Kris whispered. "Do you realize what this could mean?"

"It depends. Is it white gold? Or platinum?" Sierra asked.

"White gold breaks, platinum bends. And this is bent. And I recognize this style of backing. We had this designed especially for Willow, for ease of putting on her earrings. Her hands could be pretty achy at times."

"Wait. Just wait a minute." Joan was frowning, her fingers busy rubbing her temple.

"Headache?" Sierra asked. She looked over at Kris. "Could I trouble you for another

water, please?"

Joan waited until Kris stepped into the back room. She grabbed Sierra's hands. "Are you crazy?" she hissed. "This is going to start all kinds of rumors."

"Isn't that what we want? We're told the police think Willow's death is an accident. Having this piece verified as being part of the earring set creates a whole new situation. They'll have to open an investigation."

"They'll ask us why we didn't come to them sooner." Joan looked worried.

"So what? We're civilians, it's not like we know what we're doing," Sierra watched indecision flicker over Joan's face. "Do we...go to the police?"

Joan opened her mouth to reply when Kris set down two more bottled waters and another plate of cookies.

"So, what's the plan?" The store manager looked at them eagerly. She'd even brought a note pad and pen.

"Hey," Sierra asked, looking around the quiet store. "Nobody else is using your store for their videos?"

"Oh, people still ask," Kris shrugged. "Some even promise to buy something when they win the million dollars. But corporate still says no. No point inviting trouble."

"That's true," Joan said. Her cell phone buzzed. "Finally, it's Charles Henry." She stood up. "I have to take this."

Sierra held up her hand. "Do you want me to come, too?"

Still walking away, Joan shook her head, her phone already at her ear. "Charles Henry?"

Sierra watched Joan's face during the conversation. She could tell it was not a happy one. She turned back to Kris. "So, what happens to the bracelet and the ring now?"

"I'm not sure," Kris said. "Charles Henry bought the bracelet, and the earrings. Willow bought his wedding ring and added stones to the bracelet. Both of these items are in the vault, for the time being." She too, was watching Joan. "Who would steal earrings off a dead woman?"

Sierra debated keeping her thoughts to herself. And then she asked. "What makes you think Willow was dead when the earrings were taken?"

The older woman paled as she stared at Sierra, shock and horror etched on her face.

Apparently, she hadn't thought of that. It took her a couple of tries before she could find her voice. "So, you're saying...I mean, you're thinking..." her voice trailed away.

Joan sat back down, dropping her cell phone on the table, unaware of the tension. "Well, Willow's mother certainly is adding to the drama." Agitated she grabbed it up and shoved it in her purse. "Judith left several messages for Charles Henry. First, saying there'd been an accident. Then, by the fifth message, she left word that Willow was dead." Joan closed her eyes in frustration. "So of course, when he calls me, he's totally confused and upset. He's tried talking to her, but Judith is hostile. Apparently, Willow and her mother were not close."

"Where is he?" Sierra handed Joan a glass of water.

"He's in Los Angeles. He changes planes and his next one leaves in about an hour. He should be back in Vancouver before midnight."

Sierra checked her watch. "We should go." She stood up, and took Kris's hand.

"Thank you for your hospitality."

"Keep me informed." Kris escorted them to the door. "I'll do what I can on my end. Let me know what you two decide to do next, and how I can help." She glanced at Joan. "Are you sure you're okay? I can call a taxi."

"We'll be okay," Sierra said.

Joan nodded. "Thanks."

All thoughts of taking a taxi had vanished. There was too much to think about. The plan was to walk along the waterfront back toward the hotel. It was almost seven in the evening now. It was still sunny, with the makings of a beautiful sunset were swirling into place.

"I don't know what to think." Joan walked slowly. "And I don't have a clue what we should do next."

"Are you hungry?" Sierra asked.

"Not really. Maybe just a little something light."

"Good, I'm starving. If we stayed one minute longer, every cookie on that second plate would have disappeared." Sierra shifted her purse to her other shoulder. Then, she suddenly stopped and started patting her jeans pockets. "What happened to the earring piece?" Her eyes wide, "After we showed it to Kris." She patted harder. "It should be here."

Joan's brow wrinkled. "I can't remember, but...I don't think she gave it back to you."

"I don't think she did either." Sierra was now looking for her phone. "She said, she'd do what she could..." She punched the numbers on her phone. "I'm wondering exactly what that means."

"We could just go back--"

"Yes, but-" She lifted a finger. "Oh, hey Kris," Sierra made a face at Joan. "I left the earring piece with you. Uh huh, yes. So...I think I should come back and get it. Oh really?" She turned away from Joan. "Okay. That fast, huh? So now they know. What do you think?" Joan peered around Sierra's shoulder.

Sierra's face was grim. "Okay, well, at least the police know about the earrings. They're already sending someone over to pick it up? Okay. Hey, do you have a photo of the earrings? Really? Great, can you send me a photo? Yes, please keep us posted. Thanks." She put her phone back in her bag.

"Wow, we spent hours thinking whether or not we'd call the police, and she just got it done. Do you want to go back to Willow's house and look around?"

"And deal with that terrible woman, Gwendolyn again? No thanks." Joan waited a count of five. "So what's going on? And, do we need to be worried?"

"Kris called the police. She told them she discovered evidence of foul play concerning Willow's death, and that someone should pick it up now, because she thinks there's blood on it."

Now it was Joan's turn to stare. "Really? There was blood on it?"

Sierra shrugged. "I have no idea. But at least that makes the police pay attention to the situation and that's what we wanted. Besides, that's one last thing for us to worry about. I think we grab a bite to eat and head over to Willow's later tonight, around ten. No one should be there then."

"What are you going to do? Break a window to get in?"

Sierra grinned. "No way." She held out her hand and opened her palm. A set of house keys lay there.

"When did you...where did you get those keys?"

"Earlier today, from Willow's purse, while we were in her room. I figured we might need to do a little, ah, research, of our own."

Joan stared hard at her friend. "You've changed," she said shortly. "Whatever happened to you in Ireland, it changed you."

Sierra merely nodded and flexed her right hand. It was aching, and the phantom pain of the missing part of her finger was throbbing. "More than you'll ever know."

Dinner was delayed while Sierra had a small panic attack when staff at the concierge desk couldn't contact the guy who was caring for the dog. Things calmed down once Sierra got to talk to him, including exact instructions on the proper care for Great Danes.

"Okay, now I'm ready for dinner," as they now sat at a pub next door to the hotel. "Turns out this guy has dogs, so I think things will be fine." She watched Joan pick at her salad while she enjoyed her fish and chips. Nothing like breaded cod dipped in tartar sauce. And she traded her fries for coleslaw, so she was feeling pretty proud of herself for watching the calories. Which was why she allowed herself a mug of apple cider. "What are you thinking?"

Joan shrugged. "I'm angry about Willow's death. I mean, I know I only just met her, but I liked her. And if my cousin loved her, then she was a heck of a woman. And it's wrong that he's been cheated."

"He's been cheated? Sierra asked.

"Sure, he's forty-three, he finally falls in love and Willow was taken from him." She shook her head sorrowfully. "I just don't know if he'll ever recover."

"You two are really close, aren't you?"

Joan swirled the ice in her water glass, watching it race closer to the rim and then back into the bottom of the glass. "Did I tell you he was the best man in my first wedding?"

"So, that's how he knew about your pink and purple wedding colors."

A ghost of a smile flexed Joan's lips. "My parents were livid. But Charles Henry stood up for me." She glanced at Sierra. "It really was prettier than it sounds. It's not like I would ever do anything garish."

"Heaven forbid," Sierra agreed. "Are you going to eat your avocado slices?"

Joan pushed her plate towards Sierra. "Help yourself. I'm just not hungry. And the thought of alcohol makes my stomach hurt."

"You know, you were feeling off even before...we met Willow."

"You can go ahead and say she's dead. I'm not fragile." A large crash from the kitchen caught their attention. A few moments later, a shirtless man crashed through the swinging doors and staggered over to the bar with a boa constrictor wrapped around his torso and around his neck. Several people screamed, others jumped out of their chairs and backed away. The man grunted loud, awful, strangled sounds, as his hands grabbed the snake's head, his arm muscles strained as he tried to pull it away from his body.

Sierra and Joan looked at each other. "At least that's original," Joan said.

"Agreed. And he looks pretty hot, shirtless," Sierra added. "You know this Indie Film contest better be over soon, or no one will be able to tell a true emergency from a fake."

Walking around the chaos and the gawking crowd the ladies paid their bill and left the restaurant. The sky was dark and the city lights shone brightly down onto the street. They stood there, letting the sounds of the city surround them. Downtown Vancouver, BC was vibrant, filled with constant movement of people, and cars, and buses, filling the park and port area. Street musicians staked out different corners, some with guitars, others were singing. Across the street were two saxophone players belting out a jazzy tune. Several couples stopped to dance nearby.

Sierra missed Marcus, so she paused to take a couple of pictures and sent them to him, via text. He would love this city - once all the craziness calmed down. Maybe she could talk him into taking a couple of days off work, so the two of them could enjoy a long weekend. One street corner over was a father / son duo painted like the Blue Man group banging on bongo drums. Well, maybe Marcus wouldn't mind missing that.

They caught a taxi back to Willow's house. There were still a couple of cars parked out front when the taxi pulled up. "Late customers?" Joan asked.

Sierra shrugged. "The sale is until 7:00 PM, or by appointment. Maybe they have appointments. Oh - they're probably big spenders. Either that," Sierra mused. "Or they can't make up their minds." She grinned at her friend. "I can see that annoying Gwendolyn to no end."

"Indeed," Joan replied. She caught a glimpse of Sierra's grin in the near darkness as they started up the cement steps. "Oh boy, the steps. Did you know there are fourteen of them, up to the porch? Run up and down these steps several times a day. That'll keep you in shape."

They let themselves in. Sierra looked directly to the staircase, as if there should still be visible evidence of Willow's death. She and Joan were surprised at how much furniture was gone. The living room was virtually empty, just a couple of lamps and a few throw rugs left. In the dining room the big oak table and chairs had bright Sold stickers taped to them. Sierra noticed the silver flatware was gone but there were still several sets of china and serving pieces still available. The three-tiered chandelier still hung above the table. Bright and welcoming, the bulbs were multiplied by the mirrored pieces hanging around them, creating a full ball of light that floated above the table.

"I'm surprised the chandelier hasn't sold yet," Sierra said.

A voice from the kitchen answered her. "It's just waiting for the right buyer."

Sierra and Joan turned to see Gwendolyn standing at the kitchen doorway; her arms crossed her smile dropping off her face. "Oh, it's you two. What are you doing here?"

"I'm still considering the monkey head doorknocker," Sierra said.

"And I'm here to look around," Joan replied coolly. Gwendolyn's eyebrows shot up. "Seeing if there's anything I'd like to purchase."

Gwendolyn relaxed, but she didn't offer any smiles. "You don't have that dog with you, do you?"

Joan looked at Sierra. "You didn't bring him in, did you?"

Sierra looked dumbfounded. "No, not into the dining room. I thought you were going to bring him. He must still be in the living room."

"You brought it into the house?" Gwendolyn pushed past them, arms pumping, white-gloved fists clenched. "I told you..." She stopped in the nearly empty living room. Slowly she turned and walked back into the dining room. "Very funny, ladies. Now, if there's nothing else? I have work to do."

"Looks like it was a successful first day," she swung open the glass cupboard for a closer look at a crystal pitcher. Pulling it out slowly she held it up to the light. As it sat in her palm, her fingers curled up and cupped the base of the pitcher, leaving a set of greasy fingerprints. After putting it back on the shelf she looked regretfully at Sierra. "It's bigger than I want." Joan turned to Gwendolyn and pouted. "Don't worry, I'll keep looking, I'm sure there's something I'd like."

Their eyes locked. Sierra could tell a message was being sent and received, and she was glad they weren't sending it to her.

"Certainly," Gwendolyn said. "I'm sure you'll find several...interesting things." She pulled at cloth from a small pile on the counter, took the pitcher out of the cupboard and wiped off Joan's fingerprints.

Joan's face remained neutral, until she got a good look at the cleaning cloth busy in Gwendolyn's hands. A sharp gasp, and her eyes narrowed. "What did you do to that quilt? It wasn't yours to cut up." She grabbed the fabric out of the woman's hands. "It belongs to Charles Henry, it was made by his mother. And it was on Willow's bed this morning."

She shoved the fabric towards Sierra. "Look what she's done, she's destroyed a family heirloom." Shaking with anger now, Joan stepped toward Gwendolyn holding the swatch of quilt up to her face. "You will gather up every single piece of this quilt and you will put them in a bag. And they better be clean. Charles Henry will not be pleased when he sees what you have done."

"Well, Charles Henry isn't here, is he?" Gwendolyn smirked at Joan. "Willow's mother gave me permission to do whatever I wanted with the rest of her personal things. This is so unfortunate. I had no idea the quilt wasn't hers."

Joan flipped the piece of fabric over, now showing the embroidered signature of her aunt and then flicked it at Gwendolyn's face. It didn't hurt her, but the insult made Gwendolyn's face flush deep red. "Willow's fiancé will be here soon enough. And I doubt it's going to be a happy reunion for you two. And I still expect those quilt pieces gathered and in a bag by morning, or I'll be leaving comments about you and your company all over social media."

Sierra stepped back and held her breath. The two women in front of her were ready to tear out each other's throats. This was not going to end well. The pager at Gwendolyn's waist suddenly blasted to life with static. Startled, Sierra jumped, knocking over a wine decanter. She caught it before it fell to the floor. A second later, Bernice's voice came over the speaker. "I'm finished loading the buyer's car. How much longer are you going to be?"

"On my way, just let me clear the place and lock the front door," Gwendolyn replied, her eyes never leaving Joan's face.

"Oh, don't bother," Sierra replied, as she pulled Joan towards the front door. "We'll see ourselves out." Before closing the door behind her, she couldn't resist one last remark. "I'll be back for the doorknocker."

"And we'll be bringing Charles Henry with us," added Joan, eyes narrowed, her jaw fixed tight. She looked ready to throw the first punch. The door slammed behind them, the dead bolt making a final click.

“Okay. What the hell was that all about?" Sierra demanded. They were walking slowly away from the house.

Joan dabbed at her eyes. "I couldn't help it. She destroyed the quilt. On purpose. It was wall art, for heaven's sake. It took Aunt Clarice months to make it. It's one of a kind. Irreplaceable." Tears started falling. "Charles Henry wouldn't have given that to Willow unless he truly loved her. I can't prove it, yet, but I believe Gwendolyn destroyed Willow too."

Frustrated now, Joan rummaged in her purse for a tissue. "Damn it, I wasn't going to let that bitch make me cry." The porch lights shut off, forcing Sierra and Joan to move carefully as their eyes adjusted to sudden darkness. Falling down the steps was not on their agenda. “Fourteen steps, right?” Sierra hung onto Joan until they reached the sidewalk.

On the other side of the door Gwendolyn concentrated on easing the tension out of her face. Everyone knew stress caused wrinkles. She pulled a slim burner cell phone out of her pocket. Apparently, it was time to cause stress for somebody else. Her call was short and to the point and executed in fluent French Canadian.

~~~
~~~

Sierra gently hugged her friend as they made their way to the car. "She isn't making you cry. You're crying for Charles Henry. You know how much pain he's in. And, that's because you love him."

Joan wadded up her wet tissue and accepted another fresh one from Sierra. "Thanks. Still, I know that bitch is guilty. I could tell by the way she gloated when she pulled out that quilt piece to wipe off my prints." She stopped, facing Sierra. "I want to prove she killed Willow, and I'm not leaving Vancouver until I do." She took a deep breath, held it a few seconds and then released it. "Did you happen to grab that one quilt piece she used? On the pitcher?"

Sierra eyed her friend steadily and pulled the fabric square out of her purse, waved it a moment and then tucked it back. "Maybe with Charles Henry's help we can speed up what Kris started. The police will have to take a look at Gwendolyn." Sierra pulled out her cell phone. "It's too early to go to the airport, we should head back to the hotel. Let's make some notes and set a plan." She caught Joan's curious look. "What? I'm calling for a taxi." Twenty minutes later they were dropped off at the front lobby.

Chapter FIVE

"Seriously, you're insisting we take the Sky Train back to the airport?" Joan was complaining. They'd spent an hour soaking their feet in the hot tub, on the eighth floor of the hotel, next to the swimming pool. Talking back and forth, they were no closer to a plan than when they started. Joan's biggest suggestion was to wait for Charles Henry. Now Sierra had them walking the four blocks over to the downtown station.

Sierra ignored Joan's question. "We have plenty of time. No point in getting there too early. I can't recall you ever mentioning your cousin Charles Henry before this trip." Arriving at the now familiar kiosk Sierra slid her credit card into the ticket machine slot and bought their tickets. "Why are we waiting for your cousin? You're always the one who wants to lead the charge."

"I know. But this chick is different. I really believe she'll do anything she can to get her way, or to make sure things go her way."

"She sounds like you," Sierra replied, as they entered a nearly empty train car. She sat down next to Joan and glanced at the map posted above the windows, they'd be at the airport in about 25 minutes.

"No. I'm direct. She's devious. The quilt is a perfect example. There's no way anyone, working in estate sales or antiques, could *not* know the value of that quilt, either the sentimental value or monetary value. Gwendolyn is just a plain psychopath."

"Which means, you think she's dangerous."

"Oh, yeah. Today the quilt. Tomorrow, somebody's rabbit." Joan sighed. "This was the last thing I ever expected. I am totally off my game." They rode past the next two stops in silence; the different neighborhoods creating patchworks of light as they traveled through the large city.

"Are you going to tell me what's up between you and Max?"

"No." Joan looked over at her friend and relented a bit. "All I will say is that he broke a serious promise to me."

"But..." Sierra started.

"No. Don't bother asking. I'm not telling. Enough." Joan grabbed a rail, leaning her forehead against it and closed her eyes. "Let's talk about what we can do about this situation."

"You do know that pole is covered with germs, right?"

Joan jerked back, giving Sierra a baleful look. "Way too much information." She looked down at her hands. "What am I supposed to do about it now?"

Sierra reached into her purse and pulled out a packaged wet-wipe. She handed it to Joan.

"You're really turning into a Mary Poppins, aren't you?"

She looked at her travel bag, it was the same ugly one Marcus had given her for the Ireland trip. "I'm finally getting used to all the pockets. And this grayish brown fabric does hide the dirt, just as Marcus said it would." Sierra leaned gently into Joan. "I hate it when Marcus is right," she whispered. They both smiled.

Finally, with the airport being the last stop, Sierra and Joan stood, waiting for the train to come to a complete stop. They let the two couples pushing multiple bags of luggage off first. "Would you look at them," Sierra whispered. "They look like such tourists." Joan jabbed her in the ribs with an elbow. It didn't stop Sierra from laughing. They quickly down the hallway into the terminal.

"Where's the Arrivals display board?" Joan asked.

"Over here," Sierra pointed towards a crowd of passengers staring at the boards. "Where's he coming in from?"

"On United, out of Los Angeles. Flight 472."

"Flight 472?" A young woman holding a baby walked over to them. The baby was cranky, and kept fidgeting, throwing its head back to escape the woman's tight hold. "Sorry, my little girl is overtired, we've been waiting for her daddy."

"How old is she?" Sierra asked.

The mother sighed as she jiggled the child. "Eleven months, not quite walking yet."

"May I hold her?" Sierra asked. Holding her arms out, the child leaned into Sierra's arms. The child stopped fussing, and began poking at Sierra's earrings.

"Thanks," the woman replied. "Hand her back when she gets too heavy." She turned to Joan. "I just spoke to a United rep. There's an alert on Flight 472, and it's being rerouted to Seattle." Her face crumpled, and she lifted her hands to her mouth.

"What's wrong? What kind of an alert? My cousin is on that plane." Joan's stomach hurt, suddenly, like she'd been kicked.

"Bomb threat," she whispered. "And my husband is on that flight." Tears welled in her eyes and started tracking down her cheeks. Joan reached over and grabbed the young mother into her arms and hugged her. Sierra turned away, with the baby in her arms and walked over to a water fountain.

Joan held the young woman, gently rubbing her back while she sobbed, feeling her determination grow. Not just anger, but a need for a plan. She had no doubt Gwendolyn was behind this, perhaps calling in the bomb threat herself. They'd never be able to prove it, but that didn't mean she was wrong.

Keeping an eye on Sierra, she watched her friend and the baby play at the water fountain. Sierra pushed the button so the water arc rose high into the stainless steel bowl. The toddler giggled, waving her fingers through the cool liquid.

This threat would keep Charles Henry from arriving back in Vancouver any time soon. Once the plane landed in Seattle, who knew how long it would be before the passengers would be allowed to disperse. Would they all be interviewed? Would each passenger have to come up with a list of people they thought would do something like this? Did Charles Henry have any idea that Gwendolyn could do this? So many questions, she thought, so little time to find the answers.

Sierra walked back over to the young woman. The toddler immediately reached for her mother. Giving her back, Sierra sighed, playing with a baby was always fun, she'd been doing it for years with her nieces and nephews.

The woman waved at an older couple walking towards them. "My parents are here." She grabbed Joan's hands tightly, "Thanks for the hug. I hope you can talk to your cousin soon." She offered a watery smile just before being enveloped in a large bear hug from her dad while her mother grabbed up the baby, smothering her in kisses.

Sierra and Joan made their way to the ticket counter. "Hello," Joan said. "My cousin, Charles Henry Bishop is on flight 472 out of Los Angeles. We've been told the flight was diverted to Seattle. Is this correct?"

The staffer looked up from her screen. "Just a minute. Let me check." Apparently reading from several sources, she then looked up at Joan. "Yes, there was a potential threat called in. The airline has diverted the plane to Seattle. The passengers are being debriefed and will be allowed to leave after that."

"Debriefed? What does that mean, exactly?" Joan asked.

The woman sighed. "Well, most likely everyone on that flight will be interviewed to see if a connection can be found between a passenger and the threat."

Sierra eyebrows rose. "Sounds like that can take a while."

The woman at the counter nodded. "Most likely, this will take all night. I doubt you'll be able to talk to your cousin until tomorrow morning."

Joan's shoulders sagged. "Thanks for your help," she said, and backed away from the counter.

Sierra waited until they were out of earshot before she spoke. "There's no way this is a coincidence." Joan merely nodded.

They started walking towards the entrance to the Sky Train station. Joan appeared lost in thought. Sierra opened her mouth to ask a question when Joan suddenly stopped, her arms now crossed, a serious look on her face. "You know, I underestimated Gwendolyn. I haven't come across someone like her in a long time."

"So you believe she called in the bomb threat? But why?"

"Of course she did. It's a brilliant move. And she did it to keep me from talking to Charles Henry. And to keep Charles Henry and me from confronting her, together."

"And now we do...what?"

"Now we go back to the hotel and pack."

"Pack? We're leaving?" Sierra wasn't sure she heard her friend correctly. "But what about finding justice for Willow?"

"Oh, we're not leaving for home. We're using the Sea to Sky train passes, as originally planned, and spending the weekend at Whistler Lodge."

"To do what? Exactly?" Sierra asked.

"I'm not letting this bitch beat me. We're setting a trap."

Sierra could feel her jaw drop. "Excuse me, but what about your 'promise' to Marcus that we stay out of trouble?"

"No, no, I'm sure you misunderstood me. I said, we wouldn't *start* any trouble. Totally different."

A slow smile grew on Sierra's face. "I knew there was a reason why we're friends." She held up her right hand to high five Joan, the scars on her palm, visible under the fluorescent lighting. Her smile faded as Joan stared at her hand. Sierra's face grew serious. "We'll need to be very careful."

"Of course," Joan said. "We're doing this together."

"What about my new puppy?" Sierra asked.

"What new-? Oh. The dog stays in town."

"You don't think the lodge will let me bring the dog?"

"No. I think the train staff will not let you bring the dog. He's a puppy, a huge puppy, and he's not house trained, or crate trained."

"Details," mumbled Sierra. They had started walking again and were finally on the platform. "It's almost midnight. How soon do we leave in the morning?" She was starting to drag. It had been a long, stressful day.

"We'll be picked up at 8:30am."

"Oh boy," Sierra said glumly. "How come you're starting to perk up and I'm exhausted?"

"Don't be such a whiner. You can sleep on the train."

Sierra knew her friend, she could practically see Joan's mind racing as her eyes focused on the lights of the city. This game of 'cat and mouse" was just beginning. Did Joan realize she'd become the new target? Sierra was determined to make sure Joan didn't end up dead too, like Willow.

Chapter SIX

Gwendolyn checked her watch and laughed to herself. Cousin Joan and friend should have received the bad news by now. Whatever will those poor little busybodies do now? As for Charles Henry, he'd be lucky to make it back to Vancouver within the next 24 hours. She tapped her screen to save her files and shut her laptop. She shoved it in her bag. Clearing the receipts off the dining room table brought a smile. It had been a very successful day.

She finished writing up the deposit, and placed it on top of the stack of checks. After securing it and the checks with a paperclip, she pocketed the cash. Just a little extra, she thought. After all, she deserved it.

A loud cough made her look up. Rupert and Bernice were watching her from the kitchen doorway. Neither of them looked happy. "You know," Rupert said, "some of that cash belongs to us."

"Oh please, you'll get your cut." Gwendolyn shoved the checks into a black bank bag. "Here, why don't you two go make the night deposit?"

Bernice shook her head. "I'm leaving so I can make the last ferry back to Victoria."

Gwendolyn sighed. "Just as well, you need to pack a bag for a couple of days."

"And do what?" Bernice asked sullenly. "Go spy on the two Americans?"

"Why not? They like you. You bonded well with the brunette because of that damn dog."

"Gwendolyn, what are you up to now?" Rupert asked. Normally he'd rather not know, but he knew he was becoming more of an accomplice, and knowing Gwen, she'd hang everything on him. And the family would believe her. "Willow's dead. She fell down the stairs. That should be enough for you."

"There's no such thing, as 'just enough'. You should know that." Gwendolyn laughed. "Lighten up you two. Tomorrow is the last day of this estate sale. We'll cart up what's left for Willow's mother and be done with this scene."

"So, why am I packing a bag?" Bernice leaned against the wall, her arms crossed, and eyes narrowed and staring at Gwendolyn.

"I'm sending you to Whistler Lodge." Gwendolyn waited as Bernice reacted to the news. "It's not a vacation. I want you keeping company with the Americans."

Bernice looked confused. "Aren't I working tomorrow on the sale?"

Gwendolyn shook her head. "No. I've decided Rupert and I can handle tomorrow. I'll be joining you in Whistler once we're done here."

"Wait a minute," Rupert said, shaking his head, he stepped closer to Gwendolyn. "What are you up to?"

"I'm always up to something, you should know that by now."

Rupert nodded, his face grim. "Yeah, I know, but I bet its not family business."

Gwendolyn met his gaze, her eyes cold. "What it is, is none of your business. You'll do as I say. I'm in charge of this event here."

"I know what that means. I'll be doing everything, including all the packing, by myself. We all know how much 'work' you really do."

"Someone has to be the brains of this outfit." Gwendolyn gave a short laugh and picked up her gloves and purse. She grabbed the bag carrying her laptop.

"So how come I don't get to go to Whistler?" He scowled at Bernice. "You two cook this up while I'm busting my ass moving furniture all day. Oh, lets have a little holiday and let Rupert do all the work because he's the big, strong man."

"Don't flatter yourself," Gwendolyn said. "We both know you aren't that big and strong." She turned on the two siblings. "This is not a holiday, people, it's part of my plan. Bernice, you're heading to Whistler to keep an eye on the Americans. The plan is to separate them, I'll deal with Charles's cousin, Rupert, you're to stay here. I'll let you deal with her friend when Bernice brings her back into town."

Rupert stared at her, jaw slack. "What makes you think you can manipulate those two to do what you want?"

"Because I can. Just like I manipulate you two." She stepped up to Rupert, reaching out to caress his cheek. "You don't want the Mounties knowing about your smuggling operation, do you? And Bernice," she focused her laser gaze on her older sister. "You don't want certain authorities knowing about your...alleged drug habit, right?" Rupert and Bernice glared at each other. Gwendolyn had her siblings by the short and curlies, and they knew it.

"C'mon, we're family." She smiled brightly. "We need to stick together."

"How do you know they're heading to Whistler tomorrow?" Bernice asked. "They seemed too concerned with Willow and her fiancé to even think about Whistler."

The slap was swift and hard. Gwendolyn caught Bernice off guard. "You will never refer to C.H. as anybody's fiancé again. Ever. Do you understand?"

Bernice's eyes watered as she responded with a quick nod. But she stood tall, the hand print a bright red stain against her fair skin.

"Any more stupid questions?" Gwendolyn asked. Rupert and Bernice looked away from her, silent. "Good. I have enough to do without having to keep you two in line." She turned on her heels, and headed towards the living room. "I will text both of you your instructions later." She pulled the front door open and looked over her shoulder. "You don't want to disappoint me." She walked out without shutting the door.

Rupert and Bernice still stood in the dining room. Neither of them seemed willing to leave first. "I hate her," Rupert finally said.

Bernice slowly nodded, as she lightly rubbed her still stinging cheek. "You and me both."

~~~

"It is so beautiful here," Sierra said, as she stared up at the cloudless blue sky, surrounded by full, deep green, foliage. They'd
~~~

just been dropped off at the train station, where they now waited for their train. Sierra felt overwhelmed. Everywhere she looked flowers in every color under the rainbow spilled over flower boxes on nearby windowsills. More of them were grouped in large cement flowerpots cared for by the city. And under the eaves of nearby downtown businesses hung large, overgrown, pots of bright petunias paired with succulents.

Those were about the only flowers Sierra recognized. She was in awe. She didn't have a green thumb, but she certainly enjoyed the view. Her reputation for killing plants was well known among her friends. No matter how hard she tried, no vegetation in her care lived more than a couple of weeks. To save face, she used the excuse of preferring silk flowers to save water.

"Just remember, its Summertime." Joan cautioned her. "Trust me, there's a reason why this area is so green. And you would be miserable in the weeks and months of gray, rainy weather."

"So you've told me already. Still, I could live here all summer."

"Are you talking about our hotel, the Pan Pacific? Or Vancouver, BC in general?"

"Both, of course."

They laughed. Joan double-checked their train tickets were still in her purse and Sierra moved their luggage into a more reasonable pile.

"I'm a little confused, to be honest," Sierra said to Joan. "I'm excited to be going to Whistler, but is this what we should be doing? I figured you wanted to wait for Charles Henry."

"That was my first thought. But I'm thinking that's what Gwendolyn would expect. I'm still trying to figure her out. And if I stay in Vancouver any longer, I'll just be overcome with rage and will have to kill her."

"I get that." Sierra said with a grin. "So, we agree she called in the bomb threat. Will Whistler be far enough away to be out of her line of sight?"

"Well, if you're asking me if 'out of sight' will mean 'out of mind', no, I don't. But hopefully we'll be harder to keep track of until Charles Henry gets back to town."

"What about Marcus?" Sierra asked. "I texted him to let him know the wedding was off, and that we were heading up to Whistler. But I didn't ask him to come." She paused to check a zipper on her bag. "Maybe I should. And what about Max? Shouldn't we get ourselves some reinforcements?" She walked over to an azalea and sniffed at the hot pink flowers engulfing the bush. "After all, we are merely reacting in defense. None of this is our doing."

"I know we didn't start it, but I'm damn ready to end it," Joan said defiantly.

"What does that mean, Joan? How far are you willing to go?"

"Willow is dead. I know my cousin. He's heartbroken." Joan shoved her sunglasses over her eyes. "This Gwendolyn...this woman, for her entire life has apparently been accustomed to getting her own way. I don't understand why, but any time something happens, it's always at someone else's expense. It's time she learns this world does not revolve around her." She paused, watching Sierra roll one of her carry-ons back and forth. "You don't agree?"

Sierra stood up straight and stretched, taking her time answering the question. "I know you don't suffer fools lightly. I know you're a tough negotiator. But ,Gwendolyn seems like a psychopath, and you don't know her very well. And, you didn't answer my question."

"True," Joan answered. "But we'll have about three hours to think of something."

They watched Rocky Mountain Sea to Sky train pull into the station, and Sierra and Joan got in line with the other passengers, to find their seats. One of the last passengers, carrying a dark purple backpack, and wearing a dirty gray wide brim cap over her eyes, climbed aboard the last car. It was three cars back from where Sierra and Joan were now sitting, admiring the view. Bernice kept the cap on to hide her face. She wasn't happy, but she was determined. She had no choice.

~~~

Rupert decided not to take the ferry back to Victoria. It didn't make any sense, not if he had to be back at the house by eight in
~~~

the morning. After making the bank deposit, he stopped by a late night grocer and picked up a six-pack of his favorite beer. Sitting at the dining room table in Willow's house, he listened to the silence of the near empty space as he finished off one beer, and then another. He didn't believe in ghosts. But if Willow's spirit was still nearby, he hoped he'd have a chance to tell her it wasn't him that caused her harm. Hopefully she wouldn't mind him sleeping in her bed since the mattress was still upstairs.

His earlier foul mood disappeared after he checked the video from the hidden camera he had placed in the living room. He had hoped to catch Gwendolyn in an act of vandalism, or theft, anything that he could use to get out from under her blackmail. But what he saw, what he heard, was better than anything he could have dreamed. And after he viewed it, he downloaded several copies to various files. He replaced the SD card with a new one. If he played his cards right, he would soon be out from under her thumb. A free man.

A sharp crash startled him, causing him to spill his beer. It came from behind him, outside. On his feet, he grabbed a kitchen knife from the counter and threw open the back door and went outside. He saw glowing orbs floating in a circle near Willow's yoga studio. He would not be afraid. He would not. Taking a deep breath he moved closer to the lights and heard soft humming. And then someone started sobbing. What the hell?

A group of fifteen women walked slowly in a circle, each holding a lit candle. He didn't recognize the song they were humming, or even if it was a song. They were mourning. It was a little weird, but they weren't hurting anybody. Rupert hesitated. Should he chase them off? He was a little awed. He couldn't think of a single person who would do this for him. In fact, pretty much no one would give a crap if he dropped dead. Except maybe Gwendolyn, and that was only because she'd lose her control over him.

One of the ladies came up to him. "Hello, are you watching over Willow's property?"

He had to clear his throat before he could speak. "Yes, yes I am. What are you ladies doing?"

"We're holding a candle vigil for Willow, she was our friend and mentor." The other ladies, candles in their hands, moved toward Rupert. "Is that a problem?" another woman asked.

Rupert shook his head. "No, not at all," he surprised himself saying. "I think that's a very nice thing to do for your friend."

"Do you want to join us?" One of the ladies handed over her candle to him. "We have plenty of candles."

"Thank you." Rupert didn't know what to think. Quickly slipping the knife into his back pocket, he reached out and took the candle. "I didn't know Willow very well, but she seemed like a very nice lady. I'm sorry for your loss." *And ladies,* he thought to himself. *I know who murdered her.*

What had first looked like a long, lonely night had changed, and he was pleased he wasn't spending it alone.

~~~

It was nine in the morning Saturday when Rupert heard Gwendolyn come in through the kitchen. There was no missing her stiletto heel's crisp staccato on the ceramic floor. The city was enjoying another beautiful sunny day, and the estate sale would be starting promptly at ten. He'd be glad to be done with this job, his life would soon be changing - and for the better. "Hey, Gwendolyn," Rupert called out.

She powered past the dining room. "Where were you?" she demanded.

He stopped on the last step of the staircase, his hand holding the railing. "I was cleaning up." He knew his hair needed washing, and he purposely hadn't shaved. Slowly, he placed one foot and then the other, down onto the marble tile. "Everything is ready," he said softly. "Take a look around, if you don't believe me." He stared down at his feet. "This is the spot where she landed, isn't it? Where Willow died in her own blood."

Gwendolyn shrugged. "What if it is? It'll probably add selling value to the house."

He merely nodded and started toward the kitchen. "Is there anything in particular we want to push today?"
~~~

"As much of the big stuff as possible. There are still a couple of chairs in the den. And I'm really hoping that old man, the one with the limp, will come back for the dining room table." She frowned at him. "What's the matter with you. You could do this in your sleep."

"This time things are different, the owner died here, in her home. While we were setting up her sale."

"So what?" Gwendolyn was becoming agitated. "We're usually doing this for home owners who had already passed. It's just a different sequence of events, that's all. It didn't seem to make any difference yesterday."

Rupert nodded, and stepped out the back door. He knew she was angry and even now was probably clenching her fists.

Gwendolyn returned to the living room and clapped her hands loudly. Standing tall while taking in a deep breath, she forced her face to smile. Her ritual always helped put her in a good mood. Something she desperately needed when dealing with the public. She needed to finish staging the house so she could create great sales today. Judith, Willow's mother, was coming in today, probably later in the afternoon, towards the closing of the sale. She'd want to see results - and the money.

Chapter SEVEN

Slowly over the course of the last hour, Bernice moved forward through the rail cars. The fact that there were several empty seats in each car made it easy for her to grab a seat, and then move again. For the moment she kept the wide brimmed hat pulled over her face. Currently in the last row of the same passenger car as the two Americans, she had an easy view of them. Sierra was busy taking pictures of the scenery and neither woman made any attempt to lower their voices. If they had a scheme or a specific plan concerning Gwendolyn and Willow, she sure couldn't tell what it was. Actually, she liked Sierra and Joan. It was Gwendolyn who was losing control.

Life had become complicated, ever since Gwendolyn found out about the painkillers. They weren't for herself. Bernice had found a way to send homeopathic painkillers for animals into the U.S. Unfortunately, despite being legal in Canada, they were considered an illegal substance in the U.S. Gwendolyn gloated constantly about the fact she had leverage over her goodie two shoes older sister.

Bernice loved dogs, especially big dogs. When Sierra had brought that Great Dane puppy into the house she was sure Gwendolyn wet her panties. Especially when she spotted the dog sleeping under the dining room table on the hand-knotted Turkish carpet.

She suddenly giggled out loud, and quickly covered her mouth with her hands. It wouldn't do for them to find her on the train. But did it really matter? Gwendolyn said to pal around with them. What could she say when they spotted her? They presumed she'd be working the estate sale, so how could she say Gwendolyn gave me time off so I thought I'd just come up to Whistler, for the day?

She had to think of something logical. The Saturday Market was in session. She could claim she was coming up to help a friend run their jewelry booth. Yeah, Bernice smiled, that would work.

Deep down, what she'd really like to do is ask the two Americans for help finding a way out from under Gwendolyn's thumb. Blackmail sucked. Especially when it meant she was forced to be Gwendolyn's grunt, for a fraction of what her time and effort was worth.

The conductor was coming down the aisle again, this time he was passing out snack sacks and offering bottled water. The food wasn't bad; the croissant sandwich held a sliver of turkey meat, a dab of mustard and mayo, covered with a single piece of limp lettuce. She also pulled out an apple and two oatmeal raisin cookies. She'd eaten worse.

Sierra and Joan were several rows up, and on the right, so their window was up against the mountainside, while Bernice, who sat on the left, enjoyed the panoramic view of ocean, lakes, and waterfalls. It was more interesting to watch the women. It was obvious they were good friends and had known each other for a while. Sierra pulled a diet Coke out of her purse, along with a small airline sized bottle of Jack Daniels, and poured them both into a travel mug she carried. She then offered it to Joan, but the older woman refused, she just sipped water.

No longer concerned if the women spotted her or not, Bernice took off her cap and shoved it into her backpack, her straight hair crackling with static. She kept it short, trimmed just at chin length for easy care.

Sure enough, a couple of minutes later Bernice looked up to see Sierra standing in front of her. "Hey stranger," Sierra said brightly, "how'd you steal the day off?"

It wasn't hard to act surprised. "Oh, hi. It was the weirdest thing; Gwendolyn decided she didn't need me. Are you two on your way to Whistler?" She cringed at her question; of course they were, where else would they be going?

"Yes," Sierra answered easily. "The rooms were already reserved, so we thought we'd go ahead and use them. I've never been here before. Have you?"

"Oh yes. I have an artist friend who has a booth here in the summer, for the Saturday Fair."

"Cool," Sierra smiled. "What kind of an artist is she?"

"Ah, she makes jewelry, like earrings and stuff." Bernice felt a little unnerved by Sierra, this woman made eye contact during the entire conversation. Gwendolyn would have been texting, or staring out at the ocean, or...anything but looking at Bernice while she was talking to her. "Are you enjoying all the views?" she asked Sierra.

"Absolutely," Sierra smiled. "Anytime I'm near water is a good time for me."

"How is Joan enjoying the train ride?"

Sierra shrugged. "I think she's mostly going through the motions. She's upset about Willow, of course. And she's also sad for her cousin. Apparently he was head over heels in love with Willow. He's still not back in Vancouver. Did you hear there was a bomb threat on his plane?"

Bernice's gut clenched. That sounded like Gwendolyn. "No, I didn't hear about that."

"Oh yeah, the flight had to be diverted to Seattle. Now we're not sure if Charles Henry is going to drive up to meet us, or take another flight."

Bernice could only nod. It was amazing; the information just tumbled out of Sierra's mouth. Did they truly not have a clue that Gwendolyn wanted to destroy them? Should she warn them? Sierra was still looking at her. Did she suspect?

"I'm going to the lookout car. See you later?"

"Sure," Bernice said. "Later." Sierra continued to the back of the car, her camera in her hand, the strap around her neck. Bernice looked over at Joan. But she was sitting next to the window, her face hidden. Bernice hesitated, then forced herself to get up and make contact with Joan. The more information she could gather, the happier she'd would make Gwendolyn, and maybe find a way to escape from her.

Slowly walking up the aisle, Bernice peeked around the headrest to look at Joan. Her face was close to the window, her forehead leaning on the glass, and while talking quietly on her cell phone. Her eyes were closed, and Bernice could see tear streaks on her face. This was not a good time to gather intel. She overheard Joan say sharply. "I'm pregnant, you jerk!"

Bernice turned, quickly backtracking to her seat. Joan was pregnant? Apparently, she was either married or had a boyfriend. She didn't wear a wedding ring, so it must be a boyfriend. And Joan didn't sound happy. Bernice weighed this in her mind. Could this tidbit of information have value to Gwendolyn? She shrugged to herself, it didn't matter, it wasn't any of her business. Suddenly it dawned on her, she'd overheard Joan's whispered conversation without her friend nearby. Did Sierra know? And if not, why not?

~~~

Once again, Sierra couldn't help being in awe of the scenery. "This place is amazing," she said, grabbing her carry on and pulling up the handle on her spinner wheeled luggage. "Where do we go now?" she asked the conductor.

"Just follow the others, everyone in this car is staying at the Lodge."

Sierra waited until Joan caught up with her. "Your family came here a lot?"

"Mostly the summers, and then the winter holidays."

"You mean, like Christmas break and such."

"I mean Christmas break, Spring break and summer."

"Do they still? Your parents, I mean. Or additional relatives, of course." She clipped the man in front of her with her carry-on, catching his heel and nearly making him trip. "I am so sorry!" she said to him. The man merely nodded at her and hurried on. Sierra kept looking behind her.

"What are you looking for?" Joan asked. "You're causing a bottleneck. Keep moving forward."

Sierra grunted with frustration. "Not what. Who. It's who am I looking for. And I'm looking for Bernice."

"From the estate sale?" Now it was Joan's turn to be frustrated. "Why?" Then she suddenly stopped, distracted by a window display in one of the retail stores. "I really like that," she said, admiring a long sweater vest with a fur collar.
~~~

Sierra stopped next to her and looked. "Of course you like it, it's just like the one you already have."

Joan peered closer through the window. "Oh. You're right. Thanks."

It only took a few minutes to wheel their luggage into the lobby of the Lodge. As they waited their turn to check in, Sierra poured them each a glass of cold cucumber water from a crystal dispenser sitting at a nearby table. "This is so nice," Sierra said.

Joan nodded as she sipped hers. "Why were you looking for Bernice?"

"Because she was on the train. I saw her in the same car as us. Didn't she say hi to you?"

Joan shook her head. "I had no idea. I just napped while you went to the lookout car."

"That was fun, you should have come with me." Sierra smiled. "Great views, fresh air. Nice warm breeze." She rotated her shoulders back and sighed. "It was very relaxing."

"So was my nap," Joan responded. "But why would Bernice be up here at Whistler when she works for Gwendolyn? Willow's estate sale continued through today, didn't it?"

Sierra shrugged. "That's what I asked her. She said Gwendolyn decided she didn't need her, and she has a friend up here with a booth at the Saturday Market. She makes jewelry, or something."

"Let's check in, and then we'll go take a look," Joan said, stepping up to the check out desk.

"Great, but first, I want some lunch," Sierra's stomach was starting to rumble.

~~~

"Oh, my gosh," Sierra's double scooped ice cream on her waffle cone was melting fast. "This has got to be the best chocolate mint and coffee cream I've ever eaten." She elbowed Joan, who was nibbling on a single scoop of vanilla. "Don't you just love all the cow stuff?" Besides the ice cream, the store also carried everything in a black and white cow motif.
~~~

Joan didn't feel the same excitement. "I think love is too strong a word to use for all this." She waved her ice cream cone to encompass the store. "It's cute, I'll give you that. But I can't say, I love it."

"Oh, right, Miss Pink and Purple."

Joan merely rolled her eyes and kept licking. She did a double take and pinched Sierra's arm.

"Ow, I was just kidding."

"No, no, look who just came into the shop. Isn't that Bernice?" Joan pointed out the slim woman to Sierra. They watched as she noticed them and smiled. Sierra waved her over.

"Hi, guys, how are you enjoying the mountain?" she asked.

"This place is amazing," Sierra said.

"Have you been over to the Olympic area yet? There'll be live bands playing there later tonight." The shop was beginning to fill with more people. It was early evening, and it seemed every tourist on the mountain now wanted ice cream.

Sierra pointed to the end of the line. "Are we keeping you from getting your ice cream?"

Bernice shook her head. "Nope. I'm lactose intolerant. I'm here to find a pair of cow earrings for my niece. She loves cows. Go figure."

Laughing, Sierra pointed towards the jewelry counter. "There's more than just earrings here. You could deck her out with matching socks, T-shirt, the works."

"How old is your niece?" Joan asked. She was wiping her hands with a paper napkin.

"She turns ten in a couple of weeks. I thought they'd make a fun birthday present." She looked around. "Where did you say the jewelry was?" Sierra pointed beyond the T-shirts. Bernice nodded her thanks. "I'll see you later. Maybe at the concert?" With a smile she walked away.

As Sierra and Joan walked out they held the door open for a mom who was struggling to maneuver a baby stroller into the shop while hanging onto a 3 year old. As they walked away Sierra took a last glance at the harried young woman.

"What are you thinking?" Joan asked.

"I don't remember going anywhere as a young child." Sierra sighed. "Not really. I mean, summertime we went camping on the weekends, and we'd go to the fair every August. But as far as going anywhere extra special. We just didn't."

"Not anywhere?" Joan led her over to a bench in front of a grocery store.

"Well, I mean, we got dropped off at the swimming pool. We went to the park. But nowhere fancy, I guess is what I mean. Not like today. Disneyland, Disneyworld, Whistler. Seriously? How can families afford it? Yet today, parents take their kids everywhere."

"Are you and Marcus ever going to try for kids?" Joan asked, softly.

"Not sure, to be honest. He had an unhappy childhood, and he's sworn to never let any child go through what he went through. I've tried to tell him we're different people than his parents, but it doesn't seem to matter." She gave Joan a small smile. "Still, never say never, right? How about you?"

"Good question." Joan shrugged. "Up to now, I've never been interested. But now..." She didn't finish her thoughts.

"Because of Charles Henry and Willow?" Sierra settled on the bench, the wood was warm under her legs, and it was pretty comfortable, not to mention a great spot for people watching.

"Their chance to be happy was taken from them. They wouldn't have had kids, but they would - should - have had each other."

"Let's go check out the concerts," Sierra said. They walked over to the staging area; the stage crewmembers were busy setting up microphones and speakers for the upcoming band. Crowds of people were beginning to gather. Lots of people had brought blankets, while others were sitting in lawn chairs, drinking beer. And the dogs. So many dogs of every size, shape and color. Sierra felt a pang of longing; she was starting to miss the big baby.

Hoover was the office dog this week, with Marcus. She grinned to herself. That should be fun to hear about. Mr. 'Every pencil in its place', dealing with a 160 pound curious, easily bored, canine with a tail that could take out table lamps with a single blow.

"I want to get closer," Joan said, "but there isn't much choice except to sit on the grass."

Sierra looked around. "How about over here? The grass is dry. We could sit over here." She pointed to a grassy area surrounded by stone planters filled with colorful flowers.

"Sit on the grass? Are you crazy? There are bugs, which means bug bites. No thank you." Joan sat on the edge of a planter. "It's not too bad, besides, we're not going to stay here all night anyway."

Sierra sat next to her. But not until she unfolded and spread a couple of the brochures over the rough stone before she sat down. Joan watched her, with a smirk on her face.

"What?" Sierra asked. "This stuff gets hard and bumpy in a hurry."

"Do you know what you're sitting on, at least?"

"Oh yeah, a couple of brochures that gives the info on the different zip lines up here."

Joan opened her mouth to make a retort, but changed her mind. "Hey, looks like the first band is about to start."

Sierra had no clue who the band was, but they certainly had a large following. Country rock, she decided, after she counted one fiddle, two electric guitars, one main singer and the drummer. Not bad, the five members had a good beat going. Joan pointed the children who had gathered down in front, and were now dancing with wild abandon to the music.

"Oh, to be young and carefree again," Joan said wistfully. Her smile seemed a little sad.

"I'll go up front and dance, if you will." Sierra grinned and stood up, as if she were getting ready to walk away.

"You go ahead and show me how it's done." Joan grinned back at her. She shielded her eyes from the sun. "Hey, look over there by the Olympic rings monument. What do you see?"

Sierra turned to follow Joan's gaze. An oversized replica of the Olympic Rings mounted near the field, looked like hard candy covered with ants. "You mean, besides all the waiting lawsuits when the idiot kids climbing all over the rings fall off and hurt themselves?"

"Yes, I mean besides them, look down on the left side, holding binoculars."

It took her a minute, but she finally spotted Bernice, watching them. "Whoops, I think she spotted me watching her, she's just turned to face the stage now."

"I don't think she got the day off and just 'happened' to be coming up to Whistler. Do you?" Joan asked, her head unconsciously bobbing to the music.

"No, I can't say that I do." Sierra sat back down, shifting as she tried to make herself comfortable on the planter rim. "Can we find a different place to sit? My sit bones are getting sore."

"Sure," Joan said. "We don't need to make this easy for her." They started walking deeper into the crowd. "Excuse me," Joan said, approaching a young couple with a baby. "May we share just a corner of your blanket? We forgot ours." She shrugged and smiled. "Just to listen to the concert."

The couple smiled, the woman waving a hand at the end of the blanket. "No problem." Joan and Sierra sat down, smiling their thanks and faced the stage again. Except now they both kept looking over to the far side of the field as well, but they'd lost Bernice. Good, Sierra thought, maybe she lost sight of them, too. She leaned over to talk to Joan. "I'm disappointed, I liked Bernice, I thought she was a good person."

"I think she is, but somehow Gwendolyn has her thumb on her, hard." They listened to the band for the next forty-five minutes, standing to stretch when the music finished. Another band was announced to start a set in a few minutes. They thanked the couple again and walked off the grassy area and back onto the resort complex blacktop. Their original bench space was occupied.

"Let's start back to the lodge," Joan said. "I want to charge my cell phone. I don't want to miss Charles Henry's call."

"And when Bernice finds us again?" Sierra asked.

"It's obvious she's keeping tabs on us, I'll bet she's reporting to Gwendolyn. We'll just help her, with a few extra...ideas."

Sierra brightened at the thought. "Excellent. I've got some great ideas."

Joan grinned. "You always do." They laughed. Following a crowd they turned onto the path leading back to lodge. A few minutes later, as they started up the lodge steps, they found Bernice waiting for them.

"Hi. Wasn't that concert great?" She smiled warmly at Sierra and Joan.

"Oh, hey, Bernice," Sierra said. "Are you staying here, too?"

"No, no, I can't afford this place. I'm staying a little ways down the road. I just wanted to make sure you two were having a good time." She shrugged, keeping her smile in place, and holding her ground.

"Well, aren't you just the perfect little travel agent," Joan said, chuckling. "This is all new for my friend, but it's old stomping grounds for me."

"We're thinking of zip lining tomorrow," Sierra chimed in.

"That's great," Bernice said. "Treetop Adventures or the Superfly?"

"Not sure yet. Which would you recommend?"

"They're both great. But Superfly has side-by-side zipping." Bernice turned to Sierra. "How is the blue Dane puppy doing? Did you bring him with you?"

"Oh, he's fine. He's with a dog sitter in Vancouver. I'm hoping they'll have him house-trained before I pick him up."

"Seriously?" Bernice sounded surprised.

"More like wishful thinking. Say, I thought it was pretty funny how Gwendolyn reacted to the dog yesterday. She's not a dog person, is she?" Sierra asked.

Bernice snorted. "Gwen? A dog person? Not hardly. She's not an animal person at all."

"No," Joan said, thinking of the destroyed heirloom quilt. "She's just an animal."

"She can be a little on the crazy side sometimes." Bernice admitted, looking uncomfortable.

"You know, Bernice," Sierra put her hand on Bernice's shoulder. "We're staying in a room with two queen beds, why don't you stay the night with us? There's plenty of room."

For a moment it looked like Bernice swallowed her tongue.

"Sure," Joan added, "We'll share one bed and you're welcome to the other. You're not a loud snorer, are you?"

Sierra had trouble following the fleeting emotions crossing Bernice's face. Her mouth opened, and then closed, then opened again. Sierra was sure she saw tears welling in her eyes. What was going on?

Finally, after clearing her throat, Bernice managed a smile. "That's so nice of you, really. But my friends are expecting me. Thanks, though." She turned to leave, but stopped. "How about we meet for breakfast? The Dubh Linn Gate pub has a wonderful breakfast. It's a little pricy, but you definitely get your moneys worth."

"The pub serves breakfast?" Sierra glanced at Joan.

"Of course we'll join you." Joan smiled. "What's a good time?"

"Ah, how about nine? " Her cell phone suddenly buzzed. "Is that too early?" Bernice sounded anxious, and kept glancing over her shoulder. "Hey, I have to go now, my friends are waiting. See you in the morning." She hurried down the steps and into the evening. Despite it being dark outside, there were still lots of people out and about.

"Who do you think was calling?" Sierra asked.

"I think we both already know the answer to that. Let's head up to the room." Joan released a long breath. "And just what would you have done if she took you up on your offer of sharing our room?"

Pushing the elevator button Sierra merely smiled. "Then we would have stayed up as long as it took to turn her from the dark side - Gwendolyn - and make her one of us."

Bernice read the texts from Gwendolyn as she walked quickly to her car. Her sister was demanding updates. Damn her, Bernice thought savagely. This whole situation was getting out of control. She would call Rupert and find out what happened today. They'd never been close, but still, they were in this mess together. She'd make him help her somehow. She still felt the shock. Invited to spend a night at the Fairmont Lodge. And she passed it up! How many times had she been to Whistler, only as far as the lobby of the Fairmont Lodge? This was wrong, and just one more reason to be out from under Gwendolyn's thumb.

First things first, Bernice ducked into the ladies public restroom, pulling out her little travel bag from deep in her purse. It held a toothbrush, toothpaste, a comb, and a jar of night cream. She had to take care of business before heading to the parking lot where she settled down wrapped in her blanket for the night in the backseat of a stranger's car she'd found unlocked.

~~~

Sierra watched in amazement as Joan shoveled another forkful of scrambled eggs into her mouth. This was quickly followed by hash browns, covered with melted cheese mixed with sausage. Bernice had been right about this Irish pub, they did serve a great Sunday breakfast. Looking over the expansive choices of draft beer at the horseshoe shaped bar, she was a little sad it was still too early in the morning to try a couple. Perhaps they could come back later for dinner and the live music.

"Great place, right?" Bernice asked. She'd finished a small breakfast of cottage cheese and fresh fruit. "I know these wooden high back chairs don't look it, but they're pretty comfortable."

Joan finally dropped her fork onto her empty plate. "Wow, that was good. I didn't realize how hungry I was. You were right Bernice, this place is great. I love the character of this place, there's so many neat things on the walls to look at."

Sierra nodded. "Yeah, I'm just disappointed it's too early to belly up to the bar."
~~~

Bernice beamed. "So, how did you two like the lodge?"

"The room is beautiful, and we have a nice view," Joan said.

"I have fallen in love with their toiletries," Sierra added. "Did you know it's specially made for the Fairmont Lodge? Rose 31. I will have to get me some more of that."

"You mean, besides what you helped yourself to from the maid's cart?" Joan said. "For heaven's sakes, you swiped at least five bottles each of the shower gel and the body lotion."

"They're small bottles, and I left a tip." Sierra stuck her nose in the air toward Joan. "So, your stomach appears to be doing better, I see."

"Pretty much," Joan nodded. "Still not sure I'm up for any alcohol."

"That's okay," Sierra said. "I'll drink your share. But just this once."

Bernice watched the two ladies banter back and forth. "You two are good friends, aren't you?"

"Most of the time," Sierra answered, sharing a look with Joan.

"Must be nice," Bernice said, her cell phone buzzing. She glanced down to read the message.

"You sound sad, Bernice, don't you have a best friend?"

"Gwendolyn keeps me pretty busy. I don't have a lot of extra time for friends."

"Yet, here you are at Whistler," Joan said, looking at her over the glass of water as she took a sip.

"We figure she's forcing you to watch us. You could always tell her to piss off," Sierra added.

"It's more complicated than that." Bernice switched the cell phone to vibrate, and now it danced across the table.

"It appears Gwendolyn is keeping you on a tight leash. Why don't you let us help you?" Sierra asked.

Pain and indecision rippled across Bernice's face. She kept her eyes on the table, and after a couple of deep breathes, she stood up and reached for her phone. "Look, you gals are nice.

Willow was a sweet person, and I'm sorry she's dead." The phone vibrated again in her hands. "You need to get out of here. Now. She's coming; she'll be here by mid afternoon. I don't know what's going on, but Gwen is fit to be tied. Now is not a good time for her to find you, trust me."

"So you were sent to spy on us?" Sierra asked.

Bernice winced. "Actually, just to keep an eye on you, which I guess is pretty much the same thing." She looked at her phone again. "I'm meeting Gwen, I'll tell her you two are zip lining later on this morning, and going to the spa after lunch. Whatever you do, do it somewhere else. If you can get down the mountain, do it as quickly as possible, that'll be even better." She grabbed Joan's hand and squeezed it. "Please. You don't know her like I do." She grabbed her backpack and hurried through the kitchen.

"I think I'm afraid to move," Sierra said, looking at Joan with wide eyes. "That was a heck of a warning. Or was that a threat?"

"Sounds like a little of each. And I think she's right. We need a better vantage point before we can deal with Gwendolyn, and I don't know if we can trust Bernice to help us. I think she's too afraid. I'll grab the check and pay the bill," Joan said. "Stay close to me and away from the windows."

"I'm glad I'm wearing clean clothes," Sierra said, as she crowded herself up against a bulletin board covered with posters near the cash register. "At least Gwendolyn won't recognize me from what I wore Friday and Saturday."

Taking her receipt, Joan put her wallet back in her purse and grabbed Sierra's elbow. Together, they stepped out of the pub, carefully looking both ways before crossing the square. "Just so you know," Joan said. "We are not running from Gwendolyn, we are merely picking the place where we want to meet her head on. Got it?"

"Sure." Sierra nodded, checking faces in the crowd. It was after ten now, and everyone was stepping out to enjoy another warm, beautiful, blue-sky day. "So where do you suggest we not run to?"

"Do you have our Peak 2 Peak Experience passes with you?"

Sierra unzipped one of the outer pockets in her bag. "Right here. Why?"

"Let's go take a gondola ride, shall we?"

"Are you sure?" Sierra couldn't see Joan enjoying this.

"Absolutely. I'll bet we can even spot her from above and create a plan to keep out of her way until tonight. I wish Charles Henry would call. I'll feel better when I can tell him what's going on"

Chapter EIGHT

It was high season for the Summer crowd at Whistler, and the amount of people everywhere was daunting. Bernice side-stepped past knots of families and managed to keep from running into strollers being pushed by young mothers who didn't seem to have a care in the world. They certainly weren't in any hurry.

She turned away from the crowd. Her mind racing, Bernice kept thinking- then just as quickly - discarding ideas that could keep Gwendolyn's temper at bay. Why wasn't she working the estate sale? Usually, Gwendolyn wasn't so hands on when she was upset. Her favorite way to punish someone was to create chaos for them, then laugh and walk away. She certainly succeeded at the last two television stations she had worked.

The village property, with all its narrow and twisting streets had become too crowded. Bernice checked her watch; she was running out of time. Turning onto a small path she found herself coming up to the parking lot. She spotted Gwendolyn standing near a fountain checking her phone, her tan leather satchel leaning against the cement.

Wearing designer jeans, strappy sandals, and a royal blue three-quarter sleeve shirt, and sporting a denim jacket, Gwendolyn, her blonde hair immaculate, waited impatiently. Of course, she looked like she just stepped out of a fashion magazine, Bernice thought sourly. She glanced down at her worn jeans, old tennis shoes, and the dirty hoodie she'd worn yesterday. Sometimes life just wasn't fair.

Gwendolyn pulled off her oversized sunglasses and looked down her nose at her. Bernice realized she was actually an inch taller, and yet, Gwendolyn always managed to make her feel small. And worthless. Bitch.

"What did you do?" Gwendolyn chuckled, "Sleep outside under the stars?" She turned away without waiting for a reply. Reaching in her satchel for her notebook, she ripped out a page and shoved it at Bernice. "Here's what I want done next. Do you know where they are right now?"

"Why are you here? Bernice asked. "I texted you, I said they were going zip lining. I don't know which one, and then they planned to head back to their hotel for some spa time." She hoped Sierra and Joan followed her advice. "What's this about?" Looking over Gwendolyn's note, she was having trouble making out her sister's handwriting, nothing new about that. Bernice learned over the years it usually didn't matter, she always changed her mind anyway.

"Where am I supposed to find duct tape, or..." she squinted closer at the paper. "Zip ties?"

"That's not my problem, it's yours." Gwendolyn started walking briskly towards the Marketplace.

Bernice struggled to keep up with her. "Gwen, you cannot expect me to keep two women captive against their will. I won't do it."

"Don't be such a wuss. Besides, it's only one of them, the friend. That's why I'm here. Cousin Joan will be coming with me." Gwendolyn stopped outside the grocery store. "Go find where they are now. And text me the moment you see them. I'm having groceries delivered to the condo."

Gwendolyn, swinging her hips and walking like a model disappeared through the glass doors. "Have it your way, Baby," Bernice muttered under her breath. "But I'm sure it'll take me a while to locate them." She turned and walked toward the library. It was time to call Rupert.

Sierra and Joan stared at the line of various people waiting to ride the village gondola. Apparently, it was a half-hour ride up to the roundhouse. Sierra could see tourists from around the world. Hearing all the different languages was fun. She could recognize some of them. Joan grumbled about all the people using large tablets to take pictures.

Well?" Sierra glanced at her watch. "Are you ready to get in line yet?" Joan's enthusiasm seemed to be waning. "If we wait much longer, it'll be time for lunch."

"You know, that's a good idea." Joan turned and marched back toward the lodge.

"Are you kidding me? After the breakfast we just ate," Sierra looked at her watch again. "Less than two hours ago?"

"We're on vacation. Let's go have ice cream."

Sierra grabbed for Joan's arm, double stepping to catch up with her. "Hang on here. We are *not* on vacation." She dropped her voice to a whisper. "We're trying to catch a murderer." Letting go of Joan's arm, she stood in her friend's path. "What's the matter? I thought we agreed to do this? You were demanding that we do this. For Willow. And Charles Henry."

Joan pressed her hands against her cheeks as her knees buckled under her. Sierra quickly half-shoved, half-carried her to a nearby bench. She sat next to her and waited. Joan started shivering. "What if we can't prove anything? What if we're not smarter than her after all? Sometimes the bad guys win, don't they?"

Sierra sat quietly, listening.

"Okay, I admit it, I don't know what to do next. I guess I didn't expect all this cat and mouse stuff, you know?" Joan grabbed for a tissue from out of her purse. "How did you do this by yourself? If you could do it, why can't I?"

Sierra sat there for a minute, struggling to gather her thoughts. Just how could she explain this to Joan? "You ask me how me how I was able to rescue Marcus? I did so because I no choice. Marcus had been taken by gunpoint. It was up to me to find a way to help him, or I'd have lost him. This is different." She poked her friend in the shoulder. "And, by the way, I've never told this to another soul. Only you." Joan nodded, while her wet eyes glistened.

"Kris already called the police." Sierra pointed towards the buildings. "There's an RCMP office right here, over on Blackcomb street. We could go talk to them as well. Or, if nothing else, lets call B.C. crime stoppers with anonymous tips, maybe we can create enough doubt to make the police take a second look at Willow's death."

Sierra drew in a deep breath before she continued. "We don't have the same direct threat here. We can leave. Right now. Rent a car and go straight to the Vancouver authorities." She tugged on Joan's hands. "It's not yet noon. We can be back at the Pan Pacific by 3:00pm."

Joan's face turned mutinous. "I'm not a quitter."

"Fine," Sierra said, running out of patience. "We're not quitting. We want to prove Gwendolyn killed Willow. Let's at least call Marcus and Max. It wouldn't hurt to have a little back up. Right?"

Joan heaved a heavy sigh and nodded. "Okay, you're right. I like the idea of more brain, and more brawn."

Standing again, Sierra texted a message to Marcus as Joan spotted Bernice. She was frowning and walking fast, her eyes facing front, her arms full of sacks of stuff. She didn't look happy. Almost parallel with them, Joan called out to her. Bernice jolted to a stop and looked around. She quickly found them and hurried over. As she got close, she motioned the two over to the side of a building away from people.

"Are you crazy?" she hissed. "I told you to make yourselves scarce. Gwendolyn is here. And she is not happy-"

"Is she ever happy?" Joan asked.

"You don't understand. You are in her way and messing up her plans. And now she wants to hurt you. Both of you. You need to leave. Now." Bernice's eyes darted around them.

"That's what we're doing. We plan to rent a-"

"Too late." She started pushing the ladies toward the village gondola base. "Head for the gondolas. Go." She pushed Joan hard. "Get in line. And whatever you do, keep your backs to me. I'll stall as best as I can." With that Bernice turned away from them and disappeared in the crowd.

Sierra and Joan walked up to the end of the line, which was shorter than earlier. Hoping to keep anonymous, Sierra gently pushed Joan ahead of her, and then took a step back. Hopefully, they looked like two separate people standing in line instead of two people, together, standing in line.

Tickets in hand, Sierra tucked one of them into Joan's jeans pocket. "Looks like we're going on the Peak 2 Peak experience after all."

"Is this a continuous thing? Or is there a chance to get off once in a while?" Joan was shifting back and forth on her feet. Still standing in line, just not standing still.

Sierra pulled out a brochure. "Well, it's in sections. Cool. This first section is 25 - 30 minutes. That's not so bad. It's beautiful up here. There is so much to look at.

Joan's shifting stopped a moment, then the momentum picked up. "I don't know about this."

The line of people moved slowly, but constantly, they were almost to the ticket taker. "You can do this," Sierra said. "There's nothing to it."

Following everyone else, they moved up to the platform and stood on a painted line, watching for the moment when the open metal chair swept them up from behind. They sat down as the back of their legs touched the chair. The attendant waved at them, and they were moving up and away from the crowds of tourists filling the valley below.

Sierra was enthralled. What fabulous, clear, amazing views. She turned to Joan as she pointed out bikers riding on trails right below them. Joan was sitting very still, her hands white knuckled as she clung to the chair. "Are you all right? Sierra asked. "Are you feeling nauseous?"

"Stop moving," Joan said between stiff lips. She faced forward, sitting as far back into the chair as she could. "You're making this damn chair rock, and I don't want to fall out."

Nonplussed, Sierra slowly sat back, careful to not to cause any extra motion. "Can I at least talk to you?"

"Only if you can do it without moving."

"Okay." Sierra carefully looked behind her. "What if I told you Gwendolyn and Bernice were behind us on this ski lift?"

"What?" Joan's voice raised an octave. "Are you serious?" Joan turned quickly, trying to look at the chairs behind them, causing their chair to jerk into a deep swinging motion.

"Whoa!" Sierra grabbed for the front bar. "No, not really. Sorry, I was teasing. You know, I've never seen you like this before. I didn't know you were afraid of heights."

"I'm not afraid of heights. If you must know, I'm afraid of *falling* from heights. There's a difference."

"Okay. Well, this heavy metal bar has been pulled down and across your lap. It won't let you fall. You need to breathe and relax."

"You need to stop being a jerk. This isn't funny," Joan responded, her voice shaky.

"You're right, I'm sorry." Sierra gently put a hand over Joan's tight gripping fingers. "I'm just so used to you always being feisty. I didn't mean to scare you." She looked out at the mountains, the close ones were covered with trees, further away, the mountains showed bare granite and lots of snow. "This is an amazing place. I bet you had some great summers here."

Joan opened her eyes. She was actually smiling now. "The family loved it here. I don't know if my parents still have the condo or not." She allowed herself a look down. "This is a great place to get away from the city. I'd actually come here again," she gave Sierra a long look. "As long as you don't force me onto ski lifts."

"Technically, I didn't force us on this thing. Bernice and Gwendolyn did. It looks like we're about half-way up, what do you want to do at this stop?"

"First stop is the ladies room. And then the gift shop, I'm getting cold with this wind. And then I'm tempted to find a different way down the mountain."

"Why? The whole Peak 2 Peak experience takes a couple of hours, that keeps us out of the way."

"You said it yourself. Bernice directed us here. I know you like Bernice. But, how do you know we can trust her?"

Sierra nodded, what Joan said was true. "I swear," Joan added, "everybody in Vancouver is pretending they're being somebody else this weekend. How do we know all this isn't just some part of somebody's little vignette?"

"If this is for money," Sierra said. "Then why is Willow dead?"

Both women were quiet now. Willow. This all centered on her. Gwendolyn wanted her dead? Why?

The chair was coming up to the first station, leveling out, as the attendant lifted the bar Sierra and Joan stepped out of the chair and onto the platform. They headed for the small ski lodge. Joan rushed inside while Sierra waited outside staring at the gorgeous view. It was fairly warm now that they were out of the wind. It was July, yet snow still covered much of the mountain.

The paths were clear, and it would be an easy walk through the patches of snow to the lookout point. Sierra was reminded of Bogus Basin, the ski resort near Boise. She and Marcus did Nordic skiing on weekends. Bogus was beautiful...but these Canadian coast Mountains...were breathtaking.

"Okay, I'm ready." Joan had spotted Sierra and caught up with her on the path. "I', done shopping - for now. What are you thinking?"

Still staring at the nearby mountain range, Sierra took a deep breath, holding it for few moments before she released it. "I'm thinking I need a word to replace 'amazing'." Sierra turned and found her friend smiling, all bundled up in a jacket, scarf and earmuffs. "Nice. But...do you really think the red furry earmuffs are right for *this* weekend?"

"Absolutely. Gwendolyn would never expect it. She thinks she has us on the run."

Sierra pursed her lips. Obviously, Joan was feeling much stronger, and she didn't want to be the one to burst her bubble.

"Don't worry," Joan said. "I have a plan."

~~~

After Sierra took a couple more pictures from the lookout point, Joan led Sierra off the main path towards a metal roofed shack that served as the machinery storage shed. Walking inside they found snowmobiles in various forms of repair. At least, that's what Sierra presumed since every snowmobile seemed to be missing parts. A couple of snow blowers, sitting side by side, were
~~~

in another corner. The smell of oil and gasoline was faint, but definite.

"Why are we here?" Sierra asked, still taking in the view of all the tools neatly hanging on the walls. "Wow, someone has some great organization skills. Marcus would love to have a garage this well-organized."

"Thank you." A deep, male voice startled them. Spinning around Sierra and Joan came face to face with a grizzled, gray-haired man. He was wiping his large hands with a dirty rag. "Is there something I can help you with?"

Joan spoke up. "The ladies at the gift shop told me to ask for Mark. Is that you?"

"I am," he nodded. "The ladies at the gift shop, aye? That would be Marci and Meredith, I'm sure. What did they promise you?"

"Well," Joan started. "They didn't actually make any promises, but they did say if anyone could help me, it would be you."

Mark rolled his eyes. "Great. What do you need?"

"I need a way down this mountain and back to the resort," Joan said.

"No problem," Mark said, with a laugh. "Just hop on the gondolas, they're part of the Peak 2 Peak."

"That's the problem. I don't want to use the gondolas. I want a different ride down."

"That is a problem. I don't have any other transportation available." Mark caught Joan's glance at the snowmobiles. "Sorry, they're being serviced for the next ski season."

Frowning now, Joan wasn't ready to give up. "There must be another way down. How about a...a logging truck? Or maybe a delivery truck we could catch a ride with? Please, this is important."

Mark scratched at the four-day growth on his face. "That's not allowed. Sorry." He shook his head. "Nope, you'll have to take the gondola to the other side...or walk the ski trail back down to where you started. You'll end up at the Village Plaza."

Joan and Sierra looked at each other. "How long would that take?" Joan asked.

"Doesn't matter. At least not for another week or so. The snow is melting, creating lots of wet, muddy areas. It's not safe, it's not fun. And if we let everybody do that, it'll cause erosion. You need to take the gondola to the other mountain." He threw the rag onto the counter, and shrugged. "Sorry I can't help you."

"Well, there goes your reputation," Joan replied. She crossed her arms, obviously unhappy.

"Is there anything else?" Mark asked, as he walked to the door, holding it open for the ladies.

"Yes," Sierra said. "Can I take a couple of quick pictures of your workshop? My husband dreams of having his garage this well-organized. This could inspire him." She held her camera up. "Just take a minute." Mark nodded, but stayed where he was, leaving the door open and waiting. Joan stomped out, letting him know of her disappointment. Sierra smiled her thanks and followed her friend. They were right back where they started.

~~~

"Well, that's just great." Joan pouted as she and Sierra made their way back to the chair lift roundhouse near the small ski lodge. Joan was used to getting her way. "I'm definitely off my game. I don't know what's wrong with me."

"I think Marcus will be pleased with the pictures." Sierra patted her camera case. "He's always looking for new ideas on what to do in the garage."

"Really? That's all you can think about? How to make Marcus happy?" Joan was still frowning. "What about us? We're in a jam here, in case you forgot."

"I didn't forget. I left a Marcus a message yesterday and told him the wedding was cancelled, but that was before we had trouble with Gwendolyn." She pointed at Joan's bag. "I noticed you haven't called Max yet." As they reached the roundhouse, it was Sierra's turn to detour to the Ladies Room. "I'm working on another plan, be back in a minute."
~~~

Sierra located Joan a few minutes later around the corner from the restrooms, in the snack shop nursing a hot chocolate. "Wow, this Canadian air has really gotten to you. Oh wait, you found some schnapps for that cocoa, right?"

"I wish," Joan shook her head. "But no, just chocolate. Want one?"

"No thanks." She sat down next to Joan. "Here's what I'm thinking. We still have to get back to the lodge so we can get back to Vancouver. Plan A, we can wait here a while before crossing to the other mountain, then wait again and then take the very last of the ski lifts down, making it very late. Hopefully she'll think she missed us. Or, plan B, we should keep going and travel while there are lots of people around, I don't think Gwendolyn can do much if there's a crowd." Sierra was on a roll. "But if they try, we can create a scene. A big one. Why not?"

Joan nodded distractedly. "This could be good. Gwendolyn seems the type that's all about appearance. If we run into her, we'll behave so over the top, she'll want to run away from us."

"So we have a plan?"

"I guess, one way or the other. I wish we'd thought of this sooner. We'll have to face her eventually, so let's make this happen our way." They both stood up, ready to take the next leg of the Peak 2 Peak experience.

"You know," Sierra said, heading towards the line of tourists. "This could be fun."

Joan shook her head. "Fun? You are a sick puppy."

"Attitude, girlfriend. It's all in the attitude." Sierra kept her face forward. But she did allow herself a smile.

They were confused at first. People were standing in two different lines, but it didn't take long to figure out why. Now they merely had to agree which gondola to take. Their choices were the regular one, with a solid floor and clear sides, which was Joan's choice. Or, the special gondola with clear sides *and* a clear acrylic floor offering better viewing of crossing from one mountain to the next, which is what Sierra wanted. It soon became clear they couldn't agree.

How about this, the employee said loudly, waiting for the ladies to look at her. "You could each go on the gondola you want. I have one of each coming right up. This way, you'll only be a few minutes apart. Okay?"

"Why didn't you think of that?" Sierra asked Joan, grinning.

"I was too busy putting up with you," Joan retorted, smiling back at her friend.

A noisy group of tourists were coming up behind them. "We'll stand back," Joan told the girl.

"Oh no, you come and stand in line here," the girl guided Joan over to the far left. "And you," she said to Sierra, "Come stand in this line, right in front of me." They moved to their appointed lines. Coming closer, Sierra could hear the ladies speaking French. Several of them moved up towards Sierra, while a few went to stand behind Joan.

Joan's gondola came up first, it had been vacated on the other side of the roundhouse and now moved slowly towards her. She stepped in along with the others. She stood in the middle and grabbed a pole, trying not to look out. Everyone else took seats along the sides and chattered excitedly as the gondola lifted up. They weren't just going up a mountain. Oh no, the Peak 2 Peak experience involved crossing from one mountain...to another. Through the air. For eleven minutes. She'd read the brochure. For just eleven minutes she'd be hanging in mid-air, hundreds if not thousands of feet in the air. Dangling on mere wires until she'd be on firm ground again. She concentrated on the other voices, and their words, trying desperately to interpret the sentences using her two years of college French. She sighed. This was just as painful as looking out the windows.

Sierra watched Joan clinging for life to a pole as her gondola rose and left the round house. Her friend did not look happy. But at least she got on. She turned and smiled at the ladies in line with her. It would be their turn shortly. As the gondola with a different colored ceiling and clear acrylic-viewing floor moved into sight, one of the ladies started speaking very quickly to the attendant. She pointed to Sierra and then to herself and her friends. Sierra couldn't tell what was being said but she knew it wasn't good.

The girl wearing the nametag Emma answered, also in French, while pointing at Sierra and at the previous gondola. The response was fast and loud, others in the group joined in as well. Sierra was beginning to feel outnumbered. "What's the matter?" Sierra asked Emma.

"They want to have this next gondola to themselves," Emma told Sierra. "I'm sorry." She shrugged.

"How many people does this gondola hold?" Sierra asked. "There are only seven of us. Why can't we share? Not to mention I'm already here, waiting." She pointed to her feet, then stood and held the gaze of the first woman who had started the fuss and crossed her arms. A tight smile sat on her face as she waited for Emma to translate.

The gondola was nearing the group. The French ladies crowded up to the edge of the platform. Sierra had the feeling not only did they not want to share, but felt a larger group should be allowed to go first. Emma was set to push the ladies back, but Sierra touched her arm. "Don't worry about it. Let them go first. It's not worth anyone getting hurt."

Emma threw her a thankful smile and moved the chain to let the ladies on. Sierra couldn't resist taking the one lady's arm. "Just a moment." The startled woman blanched, pulling her arm away. "You are very rude," Sierra said. "No wonder the French have a bad reputation. I feel sorry for you." With that, Sierra stepped away.

The gondola lifted away, and Sierra turned toward Emma. "Oh well, at least I got to tell her how I felt about her behavior, even if she didn't understand me."

"Oh, don't worry," Emma grinned. "She understood every word, believe me."

"Whatever. I need to get on the next available gondola. My friend is afraid of heights, and I don't want to leave my friend alone too long."

Emma nodded. "You can ride with this next group. It's still a great ride, and lots to see, even if you can't see through the floor."

Sierra smiled at the two couples who were now boarding the solid floor gondola. "Make room for one more," she announced. Laughing, they smiled and waved her on board.

Chapter NINE

Joan hugged the middle pole of the gondola. She appreciated the rounded rectangular little cage, now dangling hundreds of feet in the air, the cushioned benches up against the glass walls were probably comfortable but she wasn't about to find out. All of them were pretty much taken anyway, with tourists who ahh'd and ooh'd at the scenery they were passing over. Down below, way down below, Joan figured, everyone kept pointing to a creek they spotted, pouring through the mountains with frothy white-water. Late Spring heavy runoff.

Every once in a while someone sitting would turn to look at Joan, offering her an understanding smile at her hesitancy to let go of the pole. The one glimpse Joan allowed herself was from behind, marveling at the pathway of fallen trees created to make the Peak 2 Peak. She imagined that would be the kind of destruction giants would leave behind, if such existed.

A tall man joined her at the center pole. She couldn't believe she didn't see him get on. He had an infant strapped to his chest. The baby stared at Joan with large blue eyes, kicking and waving small delicate arms. Definitely wide-awake.

"Hi," Joan said, and smiled. How old is your baby?

The man smiled back, and rubbed the baby's head gently with his knuckles. "She's seven months," he said.

"She's beautiful." Joan hesitated, but had to ask. "Aren't you worried taking her up on this thing?" She waved a hand.

He looked away for a few moments, then gave a short nod. "Not the first thing on my to do list. But her mother insisted. So it's fine," he shrugged.

Joan raised her eyebrows as she considered his words. A sudden lurch on the cable caused her to grab the pole tighter, any sign of enjoyment gone.

"Don't worry," he offered a smile. "The gears are merely shifting because we're almost down to the next stop."

"So, we're no longer between mountain tops." He nodded. Joan ventured a look over her shoulder and saw the treetops getting closer, still high above the ground, but getting closer every second.

"So, what happened?" the guy asked. His daughter still staring intently at her looked interested too.

"What do you mean?"

"It's obvious you're afraid of heights. So what happened to you as a kid? Fall off the swing set? Pretend you were Superman and jumped off the garage roof?"

"Wow," Joan gave a short laugh. "That's a couple of very specific guesses. Is either of them what happened to you?"

"Now you're deflecting." His blue eyes kept a steady gaze on hers. "But, to be truthful, I jumped off the garage roof when I was ten." He shook his head at the memory. "I really thought the cape could make things happen." His daughter grabbed one of his fingers and pulled it to her mouth. Joan could see a couple of teeth. Sharp white nubs breaking through pink swollen gums.

"I wish I knew the cause. It's just never been my thing. High-rise glass elevators, lookout points, the Grand Canyon, it doesn't matter. Being this high and not in control is not my idea of a good time."

"Okay," His eyes gleamed. "There it is. You don't like to be 'not in control'. Ever."

"So," Joan said. "You found me out. And here I thought I hid that so well, too."

The gondola doors opened. Joan was completely taken aback to see they were in the round house. "Oh, we're here."

"Safe and sound," the dad said, kissing his daughter's downy head. "It was nice talking to you. See you around." He stepped off and followed the crowd.

"See you around," Joan echoed, as she quickly stepped out of the gondola as well. She didn't want to ride that again. Ever. She started to walk over to the far wall to wait for Sierra, but instead took a beeline to the Ladies Room. She'd been more nervous than she realized.

She hurried, knowing that Sierra would be arriving shortly. She rushed through washing her hands, opting for the paper towels versus the hot air blowers. Stepping smartly out of the Ladies Room she did an abrupt stop. Gwendolyn stood there, her perfect hair and perfect figure, waiting for her. Gwendolyn kept one hand in her jacket pocket and a frown on her face, Joan figured she had a weapon. Would she fire a gun in a crowd? She turned to run. Except...Bernice blocked her escape, with a carefully exposed tip of a knife ready at her side, flat against her jeans. "Et to, Bernice?" Joan said, angry at allowing herself to be trapped.

"Let's go for a walk, shall we?" Gwendolyn motioned Joan to step ahead of her. "We've got a lot to talk about."

"As long as we don't have to talk about clothes. I have a feeling we have very different tastes." Joan wasn't about to make this easy. She knew Sierra would be close behind.

~~~

"Well, crap," Sierra muttered under her breath. "Joan, where are you?" The ride across the peaks had been a blast. The two couples she'd been with were a kick. Both couples were American, specifically, North Carolina. Staying at Whistler Mountain this was the first time they'd ever been to Canada. She tried to talk them into a trip to Idaho too, but they were flying, not driving. So, Idaho would have to wait until next year. She exchanged email addresses with them, promising to keep in touch.

Standing still, with people shifting to move around her, she waited to hear or see Joan. She'd wait five more minutes, then start to worry. There was no way Joan would have gotten on the next gondola without her. However, Sierra knew if there was a man in that gondola, even only one, she would have been talking to him. Sierra was always amazed at how she did it, but Joan could attract men like bugs to the zapper light - usually with the same results.

Okay, this was getting ridiculous. Where was the woman? This was getting weird. Anxious now, Sierra moved towards the Ladies Room. Perhaps Joan was feeling nauseous again. But the bathroom was empty. Stepping out slowly, Sierra looked carefully
~~~

at the crowd. Joan had to be here somewhere, but where? Enough was enough. Pulling out her cell phone, she had just started typing in the numbers when she spotted Bernice. "Hey, Bernice," she watched the woman turn. "Have you seen Joan? We got separated." Sierra suddenly stopped, looking closer at Bernice's face. "What's going on?"

Bernice didn't look happy as she pulled her knife. 'I'm sorry Sierra. I need you to come with me."

Sierra took a small step back, studying Bernice. "What does she have on you?"

Bernice grimaced. "Gwendolyn caught me in the middle of illegal drugs. But it was for animals, not people. Unfortunately, I don't think the law will care."

"So, I take it she's blackmailing Rupert as well?"

She nodded. "Yes."

"You're between a rock and a hard place, aren't you?" Sierra asked softly.

Now Bernice's face wrinkled with pain. "Please don't. I need you to just follow directions. Okay?"

"And then what?" Sierra asked. "I know who you are, I know about Gwendolyn and Rupert. Do you really believe Gwendolyn is going to just say, 'oh, let them go now'? I don't think so."

"I've never, I mean, I don't..." Bernice couldn't finish her sentence. "It doesn't matter," she said fiercely. "You will come with me, and we're heading back down the mountain, to the village. Now."

"I'm not leaving my friend up on this mountain, alone." Sierra crossed her arms.

"You don't get it, do you?" Bernice looked miserable. "Your friend isn't alone."

It took Sierra a couple of moments, and then she understood. "Gwendolyn has Joan?"

"Yes. And you will spend the next couple of days with me."

"You can't be serious. I could just push you down and run to a park ranger." Sierra's mind started racing. "Or, start shouting that you're a terrorist and you're holding a bomb under your jacket."

"Please don't." Bernice pulled a cell phone from her pocket. "Because if you do, I'll have to make a call...and you don't want Joan to get hurt. Permanently."

Sierra stared, wide eyed in shock at what she was hearing. She tried to speak, but found herself unable to utter a sound. This whole thing was surreal. Her eyes darted behind Bernice, hoping to catch a stranger's attention. They were surrounded by families; people eating ice cream and taking pictures of each other wearing shorts and T-shirts while standing next to snowbanks. And here she stood, being threatened, and no one around her had a clue. Déjà vu of Ireland hit her in the gut. Again. She was doing this again?

"Okay," Bernice said. "Close your mouth, turn around, and we're taking the chair lift ride down to the village." She gently guided Sierra into the long line for the chair lift. "You need to smile. That's better."

Sierra complied, as her mind raced furiously for options. And at the moment, she couldn't think of any. Moving closer to the platform, she watched how high the chair lifts rose above the ground. Twenty, thirty feet? Maybe she could jump off the chair lift. Or better yet, push Bernice off. She made a point of squeezing Bernice's arm.

"Aren't you warm in your jacket?" She was hoping to feel a skinny, feeble muscled arm. Nope. Very firm. Definitely familiar with lots of lifting. Bernice gave her a guarded look. Sierra merely smiled back. "You know, I liked you better at breakfast." She turned away, and climbed the steps to the platform; it was almost their turn. She wanted desperately to make a run for it, but Bernice held her cell phone tightly, and she just couldn't take the chance that Bernice was telling the truth.

~~~

Joan willed herself not to look over her shoulder, and keep power walking away from the scene of Gwendolyn yelling bloody murder. She allowed herself a smile. At least Gwendolyn was in
~~~

jeans and a long-sleeved shirt. It was the strappy sandals that slowed her down. Frozen snow will do that to you. Joan couldn't believe no one noticed that she'd shoved that awful woman into the unstable patch of frozen snow, despite it being roped off.

It looked soft and innocent, but Joan knew better. That snow was rougher and harder than cement right now, that's what happens after numerous days of freeze, then thaw. It did her heart good to hear other people gasp as Gwendolyn slipped and tumbled onto the snow patch. Joan swore a couple of people giggled as well. So far, no one stopped her, or even gave her a second look.

She made her way to the chair lift line. Did she have time to find Sierra? Gwendolyn was resourceful and not to be underestimated. Not to mention she was a total bitch. Checking faces, her fear of being separated from Sierra increased. It was easier to be brave when you weren't fighting alone. Still scanning faces, she neared the platform. What would she do when she saw her? Yell her name? That wasn't a good idea. Suddenly, she spotted Sierra waiting on the platform getting ready to line up to sit back onto the chair. And Bernice was close, very close, standing right next to her.

What could she do? It was nearly too late. Think, think. Seconds, she had only seconds. She needed a plan. A plan. "Plan B!" she screamed, as loud as she could. "Plan B, now!" She watched as Sierra raised her head, and without even looking around she brought up her elbow and shoved Bernice, hard, off the platform. She then jumped the steps and ran for the snack shop. Joan power walked away from the crowd, who was milling around Bernice and were helping her up. She ducked around the corner and ran the rest of the way to meet up with Sierra.

Without words they turned and headed down a hallway, finding a storage room. Closing the door quickly, they pushed a metal rack of dry goods to one side, and sat behind some large cardboard boxes of paper towels and toilet paper. Sierra stacked a couple of the boxes even higher. This way, if anyone who walked in for supplies, they wouldn't be spotted right away.

"That was good thinking," Sierra said. "Yelling plan B. And just in time, I'm not sure I would have jumped from the chair lift."

She heaved a sigh of relief and leaned back against the boxes. "So, how did you get away from Gwendolyn?"

"She kept ranting, and I was tired of her threats. So I," Joan air-quoted, "'accidentally' lost my footing. Of course, I grabbed her for support, so she somehow lost her footing too, and fell past the rope onto a nearby patch of snow."

Sierra slapped her hands over her mouth and tried to laugh quietly. "Really?"

Joan nodded. "You Nordic ski. You know what Spring snow is like. It's looks so soft and innocent. But it's really solid." She struggled to keep her own giggling quiet. "She was so busy yelling at me, she didn't notice how her face bounced off the snow until she slid into a drift before coming to a stop."

"Seriously?" Sierra couldn't believe it. 'I'm sorry I missed that."

Joan smiled. "I have it etched in my brain, forever."

"So now what? Hide here until nightfall?"

"I hope not. Then what?" Joan asked. "Hike down the mountain in the dark? No, thank you. There could be wild animals on the mountain. I'd rather not run into any."

"And here I thought we just escaped a couple of them." Sierra sat up and hugged her knees. She and Joan burst into another fit of giggles while attempting to shush each other.

Sierra wiped tears from her face. "Why am I laughing?" She placed her palms over her cheeks, her teeth were chattering. "This isn't funny - I'm so scared right now." Sierra pulled out her cell phone and began pushing buttons.

"Are you calling the police? Joan asked.

Sierra shook her head, holding up a finger for Joan to wait. "Marcus, oh, hi Max." A loud voice exploded over the phone, Sierra moved her ear away. "Max, calm down. We're here at Whistler." She paused as the loud voice continued. "Stop yelling, I'm trying to reach Marcus. We need -yes, I can hear you fine, tell him we need your help--"

A sudden buzzing made Joan jump. Frantically, she started patting all her pockets. "My cell phone, it must be Charles Henry."

The buzzing continued. "Help me, I can't find it." Standing now, Joan finally pulled it out of her back pocket of her designer jeans. "Hello? Hello?" She shook her phone, frustrated. The line was dead.

"Oh, that's too bad." Joan and Sierra looked up in surprise. Gwendolyn was leaning in the doorway, pointed a gun at them. Her flawless white skin on the left side of her face was a mask of anger. Her blue eyes blazed with hate, emphasizing the horrific contrast against the damaged, shredded skin on the right side of her face. From her chin to her forehead, blood dripped, running in rivulets along her nose onto her denim jacket.

She motioned to Sierra. "Move next to her." Sierra had been watching Joan and missed Gwendolyn's entrance. Neither of them had heard the door open. Glaring at Gwendolyn, Sierra shuffled next to Joan. "Okay, now, both of you toss your cell phones on the floor." Joan turned hers off and then tossed it at Gwendolyn's feet. Gwendolyn looked expectantly at Sierra, who shrugged. She'd quickly hid her phone on the shelf behind her.

She held her hands up. "I left mine in the hotel room."

A sneer disrupted the lines of Gwendolyn's face. "Liar, I heard voices. Empty your pockets. Where's your purse?"

"I left it at the restaurant."

"Oh really? Which one?" A fresh rivulet of blood trickled across her forehead, then down past the inside of her eye, like a teardrop.

Sierra couldn't take her eyes off the blood. "Um, at the Irish pub, after breakfast."

Another person suddenly filled the doorway, unaware of the tension between the women. Joan saw him first, "Steve."

Sierra watched Gwendolyn's gun quickly disappear into her jacket pocket as she stepped further into the room.

"Well, hello again," Steve said. "I heard I could find a couple of extra diapers back here, I didn't know everyone knew about this place."

He walked towards Gwendolyn, his face filled with concern. "Are you alright?" he asked.

"I'm fine." Glaring at him, she scooped up Joan's phone and quickly stepped back.

"You don't look fine." He peered at her closely. "That's quite a nasty scrape there on your face. I'm surprised you can't feel it."

"Oh I can feel it," she glared at Joan. "I was pushed into a snowbank. No big deal, my skin just feels a little tight."

"And your hands. Have you cleaned your wounds?"

"Wounds?" Gwendolyn echoed. She stared at her hands, they were covered with scrapes, and three of her nails were broken.

"Darlin', you're bleeding. The right side of your face looks like raw hamburger. We need to get you cleaned up. You could scar." He gently took her arm and guided her out of the storage room. "You're in luck, I'm an EMT, let's find transport down the hill, there's a clinic in the village. Turns out there's another lady that needs medical attention too."

At the doorway Steve turned back to Joan and winked. "Do you ladies need any assistance?" They silently shook their heads no. "So, this other gal? " Steve continued talking to Gwendolyn. "She was pushed off a ski lift platform, landing onto gravel three feet below, spraining her wrist." He kept a steady grip on her arm, asking her questions and making small talk as they excited down the hallway.

Sierra and Joan stared at each other, and then raced out of the storage room running in the opposite direction of Gwendolyn.

They started power walking back to the chair lift. It was late afternoon, the sun hanging over the far side of the mountains. There were still lots of people around BlackComb Base 2. Sierra no longer wanted more time to explore. She did wish she'd brought her camera with her, along with her cell phone... "Wait, I left my cell phone and camera in the storage room."

"We can't go back, "Joan said. "And we can't talk to the police in the village."

"What?" Sierra stopped in her tracks. "Why not?"

"Keep moving, let's get on the chair first. Then I'll explain."

Sierra looked at her in surprise. "You can't walk and explain at the same time?"

"On these trails? On this mountain? We're not Billy goats. And besides, we need as much space between us and Gwendolyn as possible. "Fine." Sierra said, a little breathless. They moved to join the end of the line. "We did give them a little help on the mountain." Joan looked at her stunned, as Sierra smiled back at her smugly. "And therein lies our problem. We assaulted those women; they're receiving medical treatment. If they file a report, we could be arrested."

"So be it," Sierra said, suddenly somber. "All this is for Willow."

"True," Joan nodded. "But it doesn't matter, we have no physical proof of what they've done to us. They do." Joan stood next to Sierra on the platform. The chair swept them into the air as they sat back. Joan allowed herself a sigh of relief. They were finally on their way back down to the Village. Now it would be a race to see how quickly they could get back to Vancouver.

"Are we taking the train?" Sierra suddenly shivered, as a cool breeze crossed her shoulders.

"We've missed the train. No worries, I'll find us a taxi, or a limo, or something, as long as it has at least four wheels."

"So you wouldn't rent a motorcycle?"

"Seriously? Do you know how to drive a motorcycle? Because I sure don't."

"I told Marcus I wanted a scooter. Just something easy to ride to the library, or a quick trip to the grocery store."

"What does he think?"

"His response pretty much had comments about when Hell freezes over, donor cycles, and...not in this lifetime."

"So you don't think he'll surprise you with one for your birthday?"

Sierra laughed. "Not a chance."

"I understand in one way, but they drive them all over the place in Rome, Naples, and those drivers over there are crazy! And the streets are small, and yet, there's hundreds, maybe thousands, of scooters all over Italy and the rest of Europe."

"I don't remember seeing any when we were in Ireland."

Joan merely grunted. "Doesn't mean there weren't any there. After all, we were only on the west coast, we never made it to Dublin or Belfast."

They were very close now, only a few minutes left to enjoy their view above the crowd. They watched as people headed towards the Olympic Plaza; probably another concert starting soon. Sierra and Joan planned to miss it. They wanted showers, dinner, and drinks by the pool with Charles Henry. They were anxious to hear his story and tell him theirs. Hopefully, in all this mess, they could find enough information to make the police take another look at Willow's alleged accident.

Chapter TEN

Dusk left faded streaks of pink and purple in the sky. Sierra led them back to the Irish pub, where retrieved her purse. Luckily the wait staff and tucked it behind the bar. She licked her lips as she stared at the pub's bar, and the selection of beer on tap. Her stomach grumbled as well. "Do you think we can grab a quick bite to eat?"

Joan shook her head no. "I don't know how much time we have. Besides, how can you think of eating at a time like this?"

"Can I just get a beer? To go?"

"Think that will taste good with Gwendolyn's gun pointing in your face?"

Sierra sighed. Joan was right. "Let's go then. Are we going to pack first?"

They were outside near the square again, making a point of walking in the shadows. Or with groups of people, hoping they would be hard to spot. "You get the cases packed. In the meantime," Joan said, "I'll rent the vehicle. We'll check out and drive straight back to Vancouver."

Sierra started walking faster. "I'm ready to go home." Joan grabbed her and pulled her to a stop.

"We can't walk faster than everybody else, otherwise we'll stick out. We need to blend." Joan continued with measured steps, careful to walk the same speed as the people around them.

Sierra hated this. "I feel so exposed, like a sitting duck," she muttered.

"Calm down. Think of this as...hiding in plain sight."

"You're right." Nodding, Sierra forced herself to take long, deep breaths, and releasing them slowly, as she now meandered toward their hotel. She could feel the tension knots building in her neck, and between she shoulder blades, reminding her of a target on her back. Just the thought of that made her skin itch.

It only took a few minutes to return to their room, but to Sierra, every step felt like a year off her life. As soon as they shut the door, she immediately reached for the suitcases and started emptying drawers. She didn't care whose clothes were in which suitcase. She'd worry about that later. The only thing that mattered now was speed.

Joan contacted the concierge. Yes, they were checking out early, yes, they wanted a car to return to Vancouver. Ready in half an hour? Perfect. It took mere minutes to gather all the toiletries and anything else they'd been using in the bathroom, dumping it onto one of the beds.

Sierra finished the drawers and went to check the closet. It too, was cleared quickly. Working together, they had two suitcases and two carry-ons sitting by the door within fifteen minutes. Sierra looked around one last time to make sure they didn't forget anything. "Well, we are a touch early for the car," she said. "Are you sure we can't walk over to the police station? They'd listen first before arresting us, don't you think?"

Joan shook her head. "Gwendolyn is smart. And don't forget, she's very manipulative. That makes me nervous. Plus, we injured them, even if it was so we could escape. It's classic, He Said, She Said. Plus, it would be easy for them to find witnesses. Who do you think the police will believe? Do you really want to take the chance that Marcus and Max will arrive in Vancouver just in time to bail us out of jail?"

Sierra frowned at her for a few moments, indecision on her face. "Fine." Joan added, relenting. "How about we go to the police once Marcus and Max are with us. In the meantime, we have time for a beer." Joan felt pleasure watching her friend's face light up. "That's the first real smile I've seen on your face in the last two days."

Gwendolyn and Bernice trudged up to the front desk of the Village Medical Clinic. Steve had disappeared after wishing them good luck and dropping them off. At least he'd made good time down the hill in his SUV. Gwendolyn considered charming him, after all, he was tall, handsome, and had medical experience. That meant he should be someone who made a good income. But he talked about his baby, and that was a deterrent. If she had to care for a child, at the very least it should be her own. She cringed as Bernice, standing next to her, started crying, lifting her right arm and showing the receptionist her very swollen and bruised wrist. RIGHT ARM? Hiding her hands under the counter, she reached over and pinched Bernice hard, in the ribs. Might as well give her something to cry about.

Nearly half an hour later, Gwendolyn stormed into the clinics washroom, barely able to control her rage. Banging stall doors against walls, she screamed her frustrations. "Idiots! Morons!" First, the EMT guy, then the twit at the front desk, and finally the doctor. Nobody knew who she was. That doctor - alleged doctor - she decided. What a quack. No bedside manner whatsoever. Rude, distant, he barely made eye contact. He didn't care about her at all. Even after telling him who she was.

Breathing hard, she focused on her reflection in the mirror. One side of her face, perfection. The other side, thanks to Joan, reminded her of oozing, raw bacon. It would be weeks before the skin on her face fully healed. The contrast made her eyes bulge, like a gross cartoon. She was used to people looking at her, but that was because she was gorgeous. Now she was this...hideous, deformed half-human, half-freak. Everyone will be staring all right, but for all the wrong reasons.

No bandages, the doc had said, no makeup, leave the skin clean and uncovered so it could heal. And stay out of the sun. Great. And what was she supposed to do in the meantime, she asked. Nothing. He actually said that to her. Nothing. Deal with it. You'll heal. The only smart thing the guy did was leave the room before she lost her temper completely.

Her fingers stroked the cold steel of the gun, hidden in her pocket. It was tempting, so tempting. And it would have been so easy just to pull the gun out of her pocket and fire it into his face. The thought of the shocked look she'd see on his face, just before the top of his head blew off, and his brains splattered on the wall, made her giggle.

She turned on the water facet and watched the water run hard, splashing at the bottom of the white porcelain before disappearing down the drain. It reminded her of a waterfall, and found the sound of the rough water soothing. Waiting for Bernice, who would be meeting her after her wrist was looked at, Gwendolyn checked her phone.

She blinked at the name of a saved call. A message? From Charles Henry? Her heart soared. Finally! He's come to his senses. He's regretted his mistake and was coming back to her. She'd forgive him his indiscretion, in time, as long as he was willing to be hers again. And this time, he would marry her.

She punched the speaker button so she could hear the voice mail clearly. "Gwendolyn," it was Charles's voice. "You are despicable, shallow and selfish. I know what you did to Willow. I know. I will spend the rest of my life making sure you are brought to justice. One way or another, you will pay for destroying the most perfect, wonderful person I've ever met in my life." The message ended.

Gwendolyn stood there, frozen, the phone still in her hands. Her ears burned, her heart ached, and she felt as if she'd been kicked in the stomach. She could feel tears filling her eyes. But she would not cry. Winners don't cry. That had been her mantra all her life. Winners don't cry, her mother would say. Every time she didn't win a pageant, her mother would just enter her in another one. Being a runner-up never counted, only being the best. Only being a winner counted. And no crying.

Bernice found her, still standing frozen in front of the running water. "Are you okay?" she asked.

"Of course," she answered, dropping her phone into her purse. "I'm just tired waiting for you. Let's go. I need to create some havoc." Bernice leaned across the sink; using her good hand turned the water off, and followed Gwendolyn.

~~~

Sierra was feeling much better with a tuna sandwich and a small beer in her stomach. It had been a long day, without much water and nothing to eat since breakfast. Joan had a plain hamburger minus onions and the top of the bun. She still drank only water.

Too curious to keep quiet any longer, Sierra asked, "What's up? You told me you were voted Miss Martini in college. Yet this whole trip you've been abstaining. Why?" Joan didn't answer right
~~~

away. She took a sip of water instead, not meeting her eyes. "Does this have something to do with Max? And why you're mad at him?" Sierra sighed. "C'mon Joan, tell me what's going on."

"Miss Bishop?" A woman walked up to her. "Your rental car is waiting in front of the lobby." The hotel staffer handed Joan a set of keys, and gave a short nod. "Thank you for staying at the Fairmont Chateau Mountainside here at Whistler, we look forward to seeing you again."

Joan made a show of grabbing her purse and jacket. Sierra got up slowly, eyeing her friend darkly. "Don't think leaving here ends this conversation. It's about three hours driving back."

Joan rolled her eyes. "I'm not worried, you'll be asleep within ten minutes after the car is on the road."

"I hate it that you know me so well," Sierra said. Unfortunately, Joan couldn't be more right. "But there's still tomorrow, and if not then, the plane ride home. So sooner or later, you're going to talk to me." She sidled up close to Joan. "Maybe I'll call Max and ask *him* what's wrong. What do you think of that?"

"I think, once we make it back to Vancouver, we should go to the precinct that took Willow's accident report. Now that Kris has called, they're more likely to listen to us."

"And less interested in arresting us. I like that idea. Let's just go. The sooner we can get away from Gwendolyn, the better."

"Besides," Joan said. "I can charge my phone in the car and call Charles Henry so he can meet us at the hotel."

"That's an even better idea." Sierra picked up the pace through the busy lobby. She turned to Joan before opening the doors. "But you will tell me what's going on between you and Max."

"We'll see." Stepping into the warm evening, they walked down the hotel steps toward the dark, sleek rental car nearby. Joan aimed the remote and tapped a button, the car beeped and the interior lights came on. Finally relaxed, Joan opened the driver door, but a hand shot out and slammed it shut.

Startled, Joan froze, confused at what had happened. Someone stepped close to her, and a voice whispered in her ear. "You didn't think you'd leave town without me, did you?"

Looking up, she gasped. Gwendolyn. Joan felt caught in a bubble. She could see people all around her, hear their shouts and laughter and conversation, and no one knew the danger but her.

Gwendolyn laughed. "You should see the look on your face."

Sierra lunged for her from the other side of the car, but Bernice grabbed her from behind and shoved her hard against the passenger door. "I liked you better at breakfast, too," Bernice snarled in her ear. She pressed her wrapped wrist hard up against the side of Sierra's head. "I haven't thanked you for the...shove."

"Ladies, ladies, can't we just all get along?" Gwendolyn laughed. "Listen, this is how it's going to be. Joan, you and I are taking this lovely car you rented, and driving back to Vancouver." She opened the back and tossed in her weekend bag. "Sierra, you and Bernice get to spend tonight and maybe tomorrow here at Whistler. I don't think you'll be out much, but you can always open a window for some fresh mountain air." Gwendolyn glared Bernice. "You have your knife?" Bernice responded with a curt nod. "Good. Keep her out of the way, and under control, or you know what happens to you." Gwendolyn turned back to Joan.

Joan folded her arms across her chest. "I don't feel like driving."

"So who asked you?" Gwendolyn's grotesque face half looked smug, while the injured half, covered with oozing scrapes and early scabbing, barely moved. Her one blue eye bulging through all that angry red skin, reminded Joan of Picasso. She raised her hand and snapped her fingers. Another figure approached the car.

"Of course," Sierra said, when she saw who stepped forward. "Your pet Rupert, here to do your bidding."

Gwendolyn merely sighed. "Be nice Sierra, no one's calling you names."

Rupert grabbed the keys out of Joan's hand, and escorted her to the passenger side of the car, roughly pushing her in. He closed the door lightly as he crossed back to the other side and opened a back door for Gwendolyn. "Don't forget the deli bag," she said before he closed her door. She rolled down her window and he handed her a large paper bag. He then got in the driver's seat and buckled up. Starting the car, he then turned on the headlights and drove away.

Bernice and Sierra watched them leave. "I don't know what upsets me more," Sierra said, shaking her head. "The fact that they get snacks, or that my luggage is in the trunk."

"Don't worry about it," Bernice said, as she motioned Sierra towards the street. "No one cares about your clothes."

"So now what?" Sierra asked, "I'm getting tired." She moved towards a bench, but Bernice pointed down the street.

"We're going back to Fitzsimmons Trail."

"Why?" Feeling belligerent, Sierra stopped suddenly, causing others in the crowd to step around her.

Bernice pulled her aside, away from anyone close. "Because. Then we cross the bridge, and find the Holiday Inn Sunspree."

"Huh," Sierra barked. "You stayed at the Holiday Inn last night?" Bernice motioned her onto Blackcomb Way.

"No. Gwendolyn rented the room for tonight." Frowning now, Bernice started walking faster.

"So where did you sleep?"

"I slept in a car." Bernice answered sharply. "Okay? Are you happy now, Miss Nosey? Not all of us can afford the Fairmont Chateau Whistler."

"We offered you our room, you could have stayed with us." Sierra tried to look Bernice in the eyes. "I wish you would let me help you," she said.

"You are so strange," Bernice whispered harshly. "Since when are we friends?"

Sierra shrugged. "Well, we're both dog lovers."

Bernice rolled her eyes. "Oh yeah, we should make a blood pact."

"Not just dogs. Great Danes. Not everyone can love a big dog."

They reached the covered bridge now. It was dark, and apparently no one was tired. Lots of people were still out enjoying the warm evening. Sierra was surprised, but she figured after such a long winter and a cold, wet spring, everyone wanted to be in outside as long as possible. Street lamps lit the way with no problem.

"So what are you going to do about the Dane puppy?"

Sierra shook her head. Was this normal to have a conversation with your kidnapper? "My plans are to take him with me back to the States. But I don't know what the rules are about that."

They were passing the day parking lots now. Sierra's disappointment was overwhelming. She felt tired. Her feet hurt, she wanted to go to the bathroom, and she was running out of things to talk about. "Hey," she pointed to a sign. "There's a restroom."

"Forget it." Bernice snapped, her hand reaching into her pocket.

"You forget it. I gotta go," Sierra said, walking straight for the ladies room door. "It's not like you have a gun, or I can disappear from a bathroom." At this point, she didn't care if Bernice stood right outside her stall. The restroom was empty, at least Bernice didn't insist on being in the stall with her. Sierra wished yet again she hadn't left her cell phone in the storage room.

"What are you doing?" Loud, sudden knocking pummeled the stall door as it danced against the meager lock. It was Bernice. "Hurry up."

"Just a minute. What's the rush?" Sierra fumbled, as she barely pulled her shorts up before the door flew open. Standing quickly, she had no choice but to flush and step out of the cubicle.

Bernice stared hard, her eyes searching over her body, patting her pockets. "I heard you speaking to someone."

"For your information," Sierra said coldly, as she walked over to the sink to wash her hands, "I was saying a prayer. Do you have a problem with that?"

Bernice stared at her a few more moments, then shrugged. "No problem." She grabbed a couple of paper towels and shoved them at her. "Here. Now let's go."

Sierra sighed loudly. "Whatever." Bernice pushed her back onto the main pathway as she blinked back the tears, struggling to hide her disappointment. "Is there any food in the room?" she asked. "I'm getting hungry. Are you hungry?" She suddenly reached out and grabbed the arm of a man passing them. "Excuse me, is there a grocery nearby?"

"There's the IGA store, but I don't know how late it stays open." He pointed away from them. "It's over past this set of condos."

"Thanks, John." Sierra smiled at him brightly.

"Uh, you're welcome. But my name is Frank," he said, his eyes narrowed.

"Of course. Have a nice night."

Bernice frowned at Sierra as they kept on walking, and glanced back to see if the man watched them. She elbowed Sierra, "Don't do that again."

"Watch me." Sierra walked up to a woman with two kids. "Hi, do you have the time?" The lady looked at her watch, "It's about 7:30."

"Thanks," Sierra replied. "You sure have ugly children. You really shouldn't breed."

Sierra cringed as she listened to the young woman's gasp of shock as she and Bernice continued walking.

"Stop this, now," Bernice insisted. "You're acting crazy."

"No," corrected Sierra, "I'm being noticed. I don't know what you and Gwendolyn are up to, but if something happens to me - a lot of people will remember me...and you."

"I'm not up to anything," protested Bernice, "I'm just protecting myself...from Gwendolyn," she finished sullenly.

"From Gwendolyn?" Sierra was incredulous. "Seriously? Welcome to the party, pal." Bernice didn't respond, but marched Sierra over to an empty bench facing the Market Square.

Frowning, she pushed Sierra to sit down, then sat close to her, the hand with the wrapped wrist tucked in a pocket.

"Can you move over, just a little please?" Sierra asked. "It's still hot out here, and I don't need your body heat." Heaving a sigh, Bernice scooted to the far edge of the bench. "So," Sierra asked. "What happens when Joan doesn't do whatever it is that Gwendolyn wants? You should know that I've never met anyone yet, who can 'make' Joan do anything she doesn't want to do."

"This isn't about Joan, or you. You're just a bonus thrill. Gwendolyn wants to punish Charles Henry." Bernice faced Sierra, her face purposely blank. "If you would just relax, we'll both be out of this mess soon."

Now Sierra's curiosity was piqued, but Bernice, her lips a tight line of disapproval, ignored all her questions. Sierra finally said. "Okay. We're just going to sit here on this bench. Out in the square surrounded by people."

Bernice raised her eyebrows; a faint smile crossed her lips. "I can tell you can't sit still for any length of time, can you?" She glanced at her watch. "But if you can just hang in there ten more minutes..."

"What? What will happen in ten minutes?"

"Satisfaction. Sweet satisfaction." Now Bernice smiled.

Sierra recognized that look. That damned Cheshire cat smile. She'd seen it on Gwendolyn the day before. Sitting back, she pressed her shoulders hard against the wooden slats of the bench. She looked up, pretending to study the star filled sky. Something was about to happen. She could feel it. Should she stay - or should she run?

"Please don't run," Bernice said, as if reading her mind. "You really don't want to miss this."

Chapter ELEVEN

The Lincoln Town car drove effortlessly around the curves and through the darkness, offering a smooth ride down the mountain. Joan sat fuming in the front passenger seat, leaning against the door; frustrated that she and Sierra couldn't make their escape. Sharing the car with a psycho, even worse, a would-be girlfriend scorned, had not been a part of her plan. Especially when Gwendolyn was brandishing a gun. She'd already been slapped on the back of her head for asking Rupert a question. Hopefully, Sierra had things under control with Bernice.

"So, Gwendolyn, why aren't you on television? I think you'd like being a talking head delivering the news, or maybe the weather girl."

"I had the opportunity," Gwendolyn replied smugly, "I've worked at two major networks. But I prefer being the boss, not a lackey."

"I get it, too many rules. I know the feeling," Joan said.

"You don't know me, or anything about me."

"True," Joan said. "But I know you've got something planned for tonight. And for some strange reason you expect me to cooperate."

Gwendolyn pulled out her laptop and began typing, her eyes never leaving the screen. "You'll do whatever I want, if you want your friend to enjoy her stay at Whistler. Otherwise, they'll never find her body."

"So, what do you want from me?" Joan didn't like this, Gwendolyn was too confident.

"Not much." She sighed. "I'd really like you to shut up if that's possible." She continued typing, a satisfied smile lifting half of her lips. "And then, I expect you to commit a robbery tonight, in the Golden Triangle, downtown Vancouver."

Joan was sure she misheard her. "You want me...to do what?"

Gwendolyn laughed as she sat forward, her breath in Joan's ear. "I expect you to rob Tiffany's. They're holding something for me."

Joan forced herself to sit still. No, no, no, this wasn't happening. She had a good idea what Gwendolyn wanted. "Why don't you just buy it, like everybody else?"

"I'm not like everyone else. Am I Rupert?" Gwendolyn ran her fingers playfully through her big brother's hair.

"No, you are indeed one of a kind." He kept his eyes on the road, his voice calm, empty of any emotion.

Joan could see him gripping the wheel tightly. She didn't want to know what that meant. "You must want a certain item that's made with Ceylon Blue Sapphires."

"Actually, two items. You've seen the bracelet. I want his wedding ring, too."

"Are you crazy?" Joan lost her calm demeanor. "How on earth do you expect me to get away with that?"

"I don't care if you get away with it, just trying to rob Tiffany's will land you in jail. And what will your precious cousin think about that?"

Joan shook her head. "You truly want someone else's jewelry that bad?"

"Not just anyone's," Gwendolyn hissed. "Willow's. She stole Charles Henry away from me. I want the jewels. I deserve them."

"How do you expect me to do this?"

"I don't care. You will do this." Gwendolyn's voice was rising, in both pitch and sound. "For the sake of your friend." She stopped short, swallowing hard before she continued, her voice again soft. "I trusted her. I brought Charles Henry, as my guest, to one of her yoga classes. I should have known, that conniving old-"

"Willow wasn't old..." began Joan.

"She's twenty years older than me!" Gwendolyn yelled, her rage filling the car. "He refused to see her ugly, misshaped hands, how much she was...deformed." She wrung her hands, the distasteful memories haunting her. "Oh no, he only thought she was gentle, and sweet, and kind." She closed her eyes, still unable to comprehend how he could choose an older woman with such an imperfect body, over her. "How could he bear to touch her? Why would he choose her over me?"

She gagged at the thought of his most painful betrayal. "And to think, they actually slept together." Grabbing her water bottle, she finished off the contents, throwing the empty plastic bottle at the windshield of the car.

Joan bit her lip. Gwendolyn was worked up and close to becoming hysterical. She yearned to reach back and slap her, or scream in her face how wrong she was - anything to show her defense for Charles Henry and Willow. But Gwendolyn was obviously dangerous. Add a little crazy, and that created a volatile mix of trouble - especially in a moving vehicle.

Gwendolyn returned to her laptop, typing furiously. Eventually she slowed down, nodded to herself. Still planning her revenge. While in the meantime, her recitation of Willow's and Charles Henry's faults were never ending.

Joan felt numb. She slid a glance over to Rupert. Dealing with all this drama had to be exhausting. His face remained carefully blank. His eyes steady on the road, with the occasional glance in the rearview mirror to check the back seat.

The mumbling subsided, but Joan didn't dare look behind her. She took a chance and leaned closer to Rupert. "Do you think she's asleep?" she asked.

Rupert gave a slight nod. "We have about a half hour before she comes round." Signaling, he changed lanes and picked up speed. "She gets car sick coming down the mountains, so she takes meclizine with alcohol. She'll wake up as we pass through North Vancouver and back to downtown." He glanced over at Joan. "You should relax and enjoy the view - while you can."

"Any chance you can just drop me off at the next wide shoulder? Or maybe we could both jump out of the car and let it sail over the cliff." She watched Rupert's eyes widen.

"Right," Joan said. "Like that's going to happen." She was quiet for a few moments. "Did you know Willow?"

"Not really," he said. "But over the last couple of weeks I've heard enough about her to know she would have been the opposite of whatever Gwendolyn complained about."

"Your sister is gorgeous," Joan said softly, struggling to keep her voice low. "Why doesn't she just snap her fingers, and have another man drooling over her?"

"Gwendolyn, or Baby, as the family calls her, usually has her pick. But none of her relationships last long. I believe...it's because her beauty is all on the outside. There is nothing good or beautiful on the inside. And I swear," he added bitterly. "She has no soul."

"In other words, after the second date, the guy pretty much realizes what a bitch she is," Joan replied flatly.

Rupert nodded. "Charles Henry lasted three months. That's almost forever for her."

"No wonder she's fighting to get him back." The rest of the picture fell into place for Joan. "Especially since she introduced him to Willow. She figured Willow wasn't any competition, since she was older, a widow, and dealing with RA."

A smile danced on Rupert's lips. "Yeah, life's a bitch, ain't it?"

Joan opened her mouth to ask for whom? But the atmosphere in car suddenly changed. There was movement in the back seat.

"Rupert, how close are we?"

Startled, it took Joan a few seconds to realize the thin, raspy voice belonged to Gwendolyn. Grumbling under her breath, the woman was stirring in the back seat. She could hear what sounded like bags ripping, and plastic tearing.

"We should be downtown in about fifteen minutes." Rupert kept his eyes on the road.

"Good." Gwendolyn pulled a small sack from her satchel. "I have a schedule and the timing has to be perfect."

Joan wanted to look around, but she didn't dare move. She jumped at a rattling sound against her ear. "Oh, sorry," Gwendolyn sniggered. "How do you feel about false teeth and a red clown nose?"

~~~
~~~

Marcus shoved his phone into his pocket. Not again. This couldn't be happening to them again. The dread and fear he'd experienced in Ireland rushed back into his mind, his gut ached with anxiety as he raced back to his office to grab his coat and car keys, Hoover at his heels. What had Sierra gotten involved this time? Joan had promised him they were staying out of trouble.

A simple girlfriends' weekend. And now? Hoover, who had raced down the hall with his owner, sensed his master's pain, and leaned his heavy head against Marcus's leg, his cinnamon brown eyes watching Marcus's every move. Absently, Marcus reached over for his big head, gently rubbing the Dane's soft, silky ears.

"Okay, big guy, I'm heading to Vancouver, you're heading to doggy daycare." A sudden squeal, loud and piercing, startled Marcus, making him drop his keys. Hoover had chomped down on the squeaker Marcus had tried to hide from him earlier. It was a horrible shrill sound, reminding Marcus...of death.

The next flight to B.C. actually meant a short trip to Seattle first via Alaska Airlines, then an hour wait for the connecting flight to Vancouver, Canada. Marcus and Max rushed to the gate, even though they had to wait. They were anxious to keep going. Marcus kept trying Sierra's cell phone, but it went straight to voice mail every time. Tired of watching Marcus being frustrated, Max grabbed his phone from him and punched in some numbers.

"Joan's not talking to me," Max said, seeing the question on his friend's face. "But I'm sure she'll take your call."

Shaking his head, Marcus took his phone back, "Max, tell me again what Sierra said to you." Max opened his mouth to retort, but Marcus held his hand up. He listened to the multiple rings and then hung up. "Okay, neither one is picking up." He stared hard at Max. "Makes me nervous to think why not."

"What was their itinerary?" Max asked.

"They were going for the shopping. Joan has a friend at Tiffany's, plus other shopping on Robson Street. Then Joan informs me her cousin is getting married, and they were going to help with the wedding. Which was supposed to be yesterday afternoon. Except, I get a message from Sierra saying the wedding was off, and she and Joan were heading up to the Whistler resort for a couple of days." He grimaced at Max. "I'm sure there's shopping there as well."

Max frowned. "Sierra said they were at Whistler, and she and Joan were in trouble and they needed us. "

The worry lines in Marcus's face deepened. "This waiting is driving me crazy. Why aren't they answering their phones?"

Max nodded absently, pulling his phone out of his pocket again. He began punching numbers.

"Who are you calling now?" Marcus asked. Max held up a finger as he turned away to listen.

"Hey, Charles Henry? This is Max, Joan's boyfriend. There's a situation..." Max turned to Marcus and motioned for him to grab his carry-on. "Really? That's crazy. What...yeah? Sorry to hear that. We're on our way to Vancouver too, but our flight is not for another hour." Max walked faster leading Marcus out of their gate waiting area and towards a security guard. "Thanks, man. That'll be great. We should be joining you in about five minutes." He motioned to Marcus to start walking. "Yeah, we're leaving concourse C shortly, we'll find you. Thanks." He snapped his cell phone shut.

"What was that about?" Marcus limped a little as he struggled to keep up, his back was still healing and he suffered muscle spasms when stressed. Like now. He caught up with Max deep in conversation with the security officer.

"So exit through here, then head to your left, past the check in counters and look for the direction signs leading you to the chartered flights." He nodded at Max as he set his hands on his hips. "You can't miss them."

"Thanks" Max said. He turned towards Marcus. "Follow me, I got us a quicker ride."

Confused, he did what he was told. At this point, he'd ride a camel to Vancouver BC if it would get him there faster than waiting for the next plane. "Who did you call?"

"Joan's cousin. Charles Henry." Max slowed his pace slightly. "He was the one getting married."

"What happened?" Marcus was short of breath. Damn, he did need to amp up his exercise routine. He hated it when Sierra was right. "Hang on a second, I thought the wedding was cancelled."

"Yeah, it was. But only because the bride-to-be was found dead at the bottom of her stairs, in her home."

Marcus stopped in his tracks. "Dead?" He dropped his satchel. "There's a dead body involved?"

"I don't know yet. Charles Henry has some of the answers. The girls have the rest. C'mon, he's got a charter plane all ready to go, and he's anxious to take off. He's in a sour mood. If we don't hurry, he'll take off without us."

Marcus picked up his satchel again. When all this was over, he'd go buy a carry-on with rollers, the spinner kind that moved over anything. When all this was over? Who was he kidding? He was about to travel to another country, where his wife was involved with another dead body. At least Joan collected jewelry. Sierra seemed focused on collecting murders.

"Wait a minute, this is too much of a coincidence. Why would Joan's cousin be here in Seattle? Isn't he some big shot CEO that travels back and forth from Vancouver to Brisbane for his business all the time?"

Max kept walking, his eyes still searching for the correct directions. "Oh yeah, he's all that. Apparently, he has quite a story to tell." Finally, locating the correct gate both men hurried onto the tarmac to the stairs where they climbed aboard a sleek prop plane. Moments later, with the door closed and secured, the plane taxied away from the terminal, getting in line for takeoff.

"So, you're Marcus." Charles Henry offered him a cold beer. "Joan's told me a lot about you. You own your company, and you're in computer software, yes?"

Marcus frowned, still trying to get his head around the situation. He nodded his thanks for the beer, dropped down into one of the leather chairs, and pulled the tab. "If you don't mind, I'd rather discuss what the hell is going on here. How is it you're here in Seattle? I thought you were getting married."

Charles Henry's somber face grew sad. "That was my plan." Worry lines furrowed his brow as he closed his eyes. "This is all my fault. I never should have left Willow to finish things up on her own. I thought her friends could protect her." He looked over at Marcus. "I'm afraid your wife, along with my cousin, have been caught in the middle of this mess."

"I understand your fiancé died. I'm sorry for your loss. Do you know any details, yet?"

Charles Henry shook his head. "I only know bits and pieces. I was flying from Brisbane back to Vancouver, so my phone was off until I landed in Los Angeles. I was changing planes, running to a different gate when I turned it on..." He shook his head. "I thought it was going to explode with all the messages coming in." He looked over at Max. "There were calls from the police, calls from Willow's mother, and several more from Joan. This whole thing has been a damn nightmare."

"Wait," Marcus said. "So why are you here in Seattle?"

Max was sitting on the edge of his chair, watching the conversation.

"Bomb threat." Charles Henry said flatly. "As if I didn't have enough to worry about. Our flight was forced to turn around and land in Seattle. Apparently, someone called in a threat to blow up the plane if we landed in Vancouver. Some crazy phone call about declaring a protest for Quebec independence, or some such nonsense. Anyway, the plane was diverted here to Seattle. After all the passengers deplaned, we were interrogated for hours. Our passports were confiscated, along with our cell phones. They gave me mine back sooner than the others because of the messages about Willow. I was going crazy with the delay. All I could think about was Willow. Finally, I was allowed to make calls, with supervision. It took hours to wait for completed background checks on all the passengers, the whole works."

"So here it is, Saturday evening, and you should have been back in Vancouver yesterday morning."

"And married this afternoon." Charles Henry closed his eyes. "Willow and I were to be spending our wedding night at Whistler." His voice cracked slightly, and tears ran down his cheeks. "I'm forty-four years old, a bachelor. This is the first time I've ever found someone I wanted to spend the rest of my life with." He spread his hands. "And now..."

Marcus understood how he felt. That was the main reason Sierra's insistence of doing things on her own scared the hell out of him. What would he ever do without her? He looked over at Max. He'd never seen Max look so serious.

"What do we need to do?" Max asked. "I'm in. Whatever it takes. Tell me what I can do, and it'll get done." He looked at Marcus. "Where do we start? With Kris?"

"Who's Kris?" Marcus asked.

"Kris Query. She's a friend of mine," Charles Henry said. "She works at Tiffany's in downtown Vancouver. Joan introduced me to Kris. She helped me design the earrings and wedding bracelet for Willow." He threw a half smile at Max. "You may have noticed Joan likes jewelry."

Max rolled his eyes and nodded. "I think she's the queen of bling."

"So," Marcus cleared his throat, anxious to get back on track. "You think Kris can help us?"

Charles Henry pulled a handkerchief from his pocket to wipe his eyes; he could only shrug. "We'll be landing shortly. I think Tiffany's is a good place to start."

~~~

Sierra struggled to sit still. She crossed and uncrossed her legs. She raised her legs level with the bench seat and rotated her ankles, first to the left, then to the right. They were still sitting outside in the market square at Whistler. "You know, this bench is no longer comfortable. Can we at least walk around?"

Bernice looked at her watch and frowned. "I suppose."

"Why can't we go to the hotel room? At least we could get some water, relax in comfortable chairs."

"You want a bottled water?" Bernice asked, standing now, and looking around. She could hear country music from a nearby bar.
~~~

"What I'd really like is a bourbon and Coke," Sierra said. "Do you drink? I'll buy."

"Will you behave?" Bernice looked doubtful. "You're not exactly trustworthy."

Sierra yawned widely and shrugged. "If you can find me a comfortable chair to sit in, and some alcohol, then yes, I'll behave."

"Promise?" Bernice put both her hands in her pockets.

Sierra knew her captor was grabbing a cell phone in one pocket, and a knife in the other. "Yes, I promise."

"Okay then," Bernice nodded towards the music. "Let's go."

Fifteen minutes later, after pushing their way through a throng of bodies, head- bobbing to the music, they were relaxing on overstuffed couches in the far corner, furthest away from the band. Sierra sipped her bourbon Coke, watching Bernice nurse her iced tea. "So, you keep looking at your watch. Are we on a schedule?"

"Things work better with a schedule," Bernice replied primly.

"It's not much of a schedule, we sat there a lot longer than ten minutes for nothing. And you didn't answer my question," Sierra said. "Why can't we go to the hotel room?"

"It's more like a motel room," Bernice answered.

"Are we waiting for someone?"

"You ask too many questions," Bernice countered, clearly irritated.

"That happens to me when I'm threatened with a knife and my friend is in danger." Sierra took another long sip of her drink. "You and Rupert seem very close. Did you two draw the short straw?"

"What?" Bernice blinked. "What do you mean, the short straw?"

"Well, you're always doing everything Gwendolyn wants. When do you get to do what you want?"

"Ah," Bernice shrugged. "She's the baby of the family, that's the way it works. The older siblings take care of the family business. Then Rupert and me, being older, take care of the youngest, the baby of the family, especially since Mama passed away."

"When was that?"

"Right after Gwendolyn placed first runner up in the Miss British Columbia contest."

"Wow, I'm not surprised, she looks like a beauty pageant winner."

Glowing with pride, Bernice took out her wallet and passed a couple of pictures to Sierra. "Here's when she won Miss Vancouver Island. And the other one, on the finals night of the big pageant."

Sierra studied the photos, then handed them back. "She looks really happy in the first one. Definitely in her element. She doesn't look quite so happy in the Miss Canada contest. What happened?"

"She lost."

"But she finished as first-runner-up. That sounds like a great win to me."

"Broke mama's heart. Even after the winner had to step down." Bernice leaned forward and whispered. "There was a scandal a couple of months later, and they gave the crown to Gwendolyn. Still, second place doesn't count in our family."

"Oh." Music filled the awkward silence. The waitress walked by and Sierra flagged her for another drink. She turned to Bernice. "Do you want another iced tea?" The smaller women shook her head, checking her watch again.

"So, you and Rupert help Gwendolyn with, pretty much everything. And, I guess, under normal circumstances that would work. What she's doing now is wrong, kidnapping is illegal. When she's caught," Sierra said, leaning close to make sure Bernice heard her, looking her straight in the eyes, "and Gwendolyn will be caught - she will go to prison. There's nothing you can do about that. Are you willing to let her drag you down with her? Seriously?"

Bernice looked away, the napkin she'd been holding now wadded up in a tight paper ball. "She's always been a handful. I'll give you that."

"Looks like you've devoted your life to her." Sierra kept pressing. "Does she know that? Is she ever grateful?"

Bernice shook her head. "Enough. I'm tired of talking. I'm tired of you talking. Just be quiet and listen to the music." She started rubbing her wrapped wrist.

The waitress came to the table and set down Sierra's second bourbon and Coke. Sierra dug a twenty-dollar bill out of her pocket. "Here, I only have American money on me. Keep the change." Handing her the bill, she hung onto it for a moment, making the gal move closer to her. Sierra tried to show a look of distress, but the waitress merely nodded her thanks, never making eye contact. Sierra looked back over at Bernice. "What is the exchange rate now between the US greenback and Canadian Loonie?" Bernice only shrugged, obviously determined not to speak to Sierra. She pulled out her cell phone and started texting.

Shaking her head, Sierra watched Bernice struggle to text with her left hand. "Everything okay?" Sierra leaned forward as if trying to read the screen. Bernice glared at her, and pulled her phone closer to her chest. Sierra sighed. She took this chance to look around at the crowd, trying to make eye contact with somebody. Anybody. The growing feeling of dread that time was running out made her stomach knot up. She picked up her drink and gulped it down. Staring at the remaining ice, she considered dropping the glass for attention. But the band was playing loudly. Would anyone even notice?

Her heart ached with indecision. The only reason Sierra was still sitting at the table was the fear of Gwendolyn following through with her threat of hurting Joan, or worse. Even if she managed to grab Bernice's cell phone, could she still reach the police in time?

And tell them what? She had no idea where Gwendolyn had taken Joan. All Bernice would have to do is find a phone and make the call. Running solved nothing.

Did Max reach Marcus? Would he even understand her message? She leaned back against the black faux-leather couch, her arms crossed. She could feel her heart pounding, her nerves stretched about as far as she thought they could go before she cracked and did stupid.

Waiting was never her strong suit. She cleared her throat. "It's been almost an hour. How much longer, Bernice? I'm tired of waiting. What happened to the 'only ten more minutes'?"

Bernice wasn't any happier. Her frown matched Sierra's. "I don't know. Are you always this childish? Calm down, things seem a little disorganized at the moment."

"Disorganized?" Sierra thought about that for a few moments. "How is that comment supposed to be calming? Maybe we should head down the mountain to help."

Bernice tucked her phone back in a pocket. All set to lecture, Sierra stopped when the waitress appeared at their table with another bourbon and Coke and an iced tea, along with an appetizer of potato skins. "Wait, we didn't order this," she said.

"A gentleman bought your drinks," the waitress explained, looking over her shoulder, "he said the potato skins are for him."

"Good evening, ladies." A tall, good-looking man slid onto the couch next to Bernice. "I hope you don't mind. I couldn't resist sitting by two gorgeous gals." His smile showed a full set of straight teeth, so white Sierra was sure they could glow in the dark.

Bernice looked over at Sierra and grimaced. Gorgeous? But Sierra saw this as a way out, and smiled at him. "Hi. I'm Sierra, my friend here is Bernice."

Bernice glared at Sierra. The uninvited guest tipped his hat and took off his sunglasses. "Hi, ladies, my name is Jack. Jack Russell."

Sierra's eyebrows rose as she struggled to keep a smile off her face. *Jack...is...Max?* She'd go along with it. Max was here to rescue her, but who would rescue him?

Bernice giggled nervously. "You're named after a breed of dog?"

"Yep, what can I say? We had one as a family pet. Parents, right?" He winked at Sierra and shook his head slightly. "How about you?" As he turned his full attention to Bernice, she quickly shifted away from him by several inches, her demeanor screaming that she was not impressed with this intruder.

Jack kept his eyes on Bernice. "Do you like dogs, Bernice?" he asked. Sierra moved a couple of inches away as well, hoping she was becoming invisible. Jack was turning on the charm at full blast.

Bernice slowly nodded her head. Even in the low light of the bar Sierra could see her blushing. "I like dogs very much," she said softly. Jack had to lean closer to hear her.

He smiled at her. "Do you have a favorite breed?" He kept his eyes focused on her, as if she were the only person in the room.

Now she smiled, cocking her head, her eyes watching him closely. "I like all dogs, but I think I have a special love for the big dogs."

With Jack keeping the conversation going, Sierra helped herself to a potato skin. Cut in large strips, each slice held the perfect amount of sour cream, sprinkled with green onion slices and bacon bits, with grated cheddar cheese that had melted over everything. Wow. She didn't realize how hungry she was.

She helped herself to another. Max was doing a great job keeping Bernice distracted. Too bad it didn't matter, Sierra didn't dare leave. As long as Bernice could get to a phone, she could still send the 'kill call'. She couldn't see a way to take her phone away from her, not when she was sitting across the table, and kept the cell phone in a sweater pocket.

Sierra considered again about making a scene and grabbing the phone away from her. Oh, wait, she'd forgotten about the knife. Damn. She glanced down at her right hand. She couldn't see the scars, it was too dark in the bar, but they were there. What didn't show was the aching pain of a hand still healing, the tenderness and pain of torn tendons pulled during physical therapy. Was she willing to lose a little bit more, to save her friend?

And what about Max? Would he be any help? Could she trust him to follow her lead? There wouldn't be any time to explain. She sipped her drink. The timing would have to be just right.

"So, Jack," Sierra said, interrupting the story of his first puppy. "How'd you get a name like 'Jack'?"

"Actually, one of my brothers named me. Mom liked it, so it stuck."

"How many siblings do you have?" Bernice asked. Sierra noticed she wasn't frowning any more.

"I have four brothers, I'm the youngest." He shrugged, and looked over at Sierra. "I take it you were a middle child."

"You're the youngest," Bernice repeated, "so...you're the baby of the family."

Sierra could feel Bernice's energy change. She tried to step on Max's toes to get his attention.

Max shifted his feet, ignoring Sierra. "Yes, my brothers are constantly trying to keep me in line, they can be a pain sometimes, but I manage to do what I want with my life anyway." Sierra looked him in the eyes and shook her head. Wrong thing to say.

Bernice nodded. "I understand." She gave him a ghost of a smile. "I have empathy for your brothers. I'm one of the older siblings that takes care of the baby of the family."

"Well, Bernice," he gently touched her hand and then reached for his beer. "Speaking as the 'baby' as you say, I know I'm not needing quite as much sibling guidance as they think I do."

"Oh please," Bernice drew herself up, "the baby of the family gets away with murder, and you know it."

Sierra froze. Murder? Was Bernice saying she knew Gwendolyn murdered Willow? Even Jack was surprised at the outburst. He quickly recovered with a lopsided grin. "At least my brothers don't know where the bodies are."

"I wish," Bernice murmured, her words muffled as she sipped her iced tea.

Sierra opened her mouth to say something, but Max shook his head. She didn't know how much more of this she could take. Her fight or flight urge was going haywire. Do something! Her brain was screaming. Do something! Her body demanded. But what? If she didn't figure something out soon, her knotted stomach was going to throw up. That, at least, would change the subject, Sierra decided. And...it would get attention.

The band had just finished a set and was stepping off the stage for a break. Now would be a good time. She knew a gal in high school who could vomit at will, and did so whenever she wasn't ready to take an exam. Usually in the hall, right outside the door of the classroom. Could she do this? She'd never thrown up on purpose. She looked over at Bernice and Max. He had brought the conversation back to dogs, but Bernice's demeanor had changed. She looked agitated.

Finishing off her drink, Sierra had to admit she was feeling no pain. Looking at the appetizer plate, she realized she'd eaten all of the potato skins. She held her head in her hands and felt her face. Yep, her nose was numb. She'd reached her limit. Think. Think. Did she actually see the knife? Yes, Bernice had shown the tip of it, once. Sierra had no clue how long the blade was. Could it be a switchblade? Another glance at Bernice and Sierra knew she had to make a move.

"Jack?" Sierra tried to smile while pretending to be having trouble keeping her eyes open. "I'm tired." Leaning forward, she struggled to keep her head from lying on the tabletop. "Could you please...take me back to my hotel?"

Max looked over at Bernice. "I think your friend is done for the day. Can I give you ladies a lift somewhere?"

Bernice's frown returned, she pulled her hands back and tucked them under the table. She shook her head. "I think she's faking. She hates not being the center of attention."

"Really?" Max looked surprised. "How long have you two been friends?" He watched as Sierra sat up again.

"Okay Bernice, how long do you think we've been friends?" Sierra started shifting closer. "I've known you for about, hmm," she glanced down at her watch. "About forty-eight hours, give or take? I think it's safe to say we are not friends." She faced Max, speaking louder this time. "She and I are not friends." Sierra waved her hand to indicate the two of them. "We will never be friends." Bernice froze, a look of resigned disgust on her face. Her hands still hidden under the table.

"Go on," Sierra said. "Tell him how you are keeping me here, under threats, with a knife, and a cell phone, just a push of a button away from Gwendolyn, who's kidnapped my friend Joan." She looked at Max. "If I escape and call the cops, she'll call Gwendolyn, who will then hurt or kill my friend."

He looked at Bernice, amazement filling his face. "But...Bernice, you like dogs."

"Enough." Bernice's eyes glittered with hate. "You don't understand. I *have* to do this. Baby sometimes gets in over her head, and I have to help her. It's my responsibility."

"Gwendolyn is thirty-seven years old. It's time she learns that actions matter." Max's smile dropped from his face. "It's easy, as the baby of the family, to let others do things for you. It's convenient, to let others take the blame. But there comes a time, when the baby has to grow up. Let Gwendolyn take responsibility for her actions." Max leaned towards Bernice, his hand on her shoulder. "I know this, I had to learn this the hard way too. Let it go."

"I knew you were a fake." She slowly shook her head, and then shrugged. "Sorry, Jack, or whatever your name is, I just can't." In a sudden, fluid movement, Bernice, her knife suddenly in her left hand, plunged it into Max's stomach. He stood up, the knife still in his body. Blood began blossoming around the wound and through his shirt, dripping onto the leather couch beneath him.

Chapter TWELVE

It took Sierra several seconds before she could react. She jumped to her feet. "Oh my God, Max!" She looked over at Bernice, and the smirk on her face. Bernice's blue eyes flashed, and in that moment Sierra was looking at Gwendolyn's eyes. Sierra drew a sharp breath, she'd forgotten they were twins; she'd forgotten they shared the same blood. Worst of all, she had forgotten Bernice could be dangerous. "You won't get away with this!" Sierra moved to help Max.

He groaned and legs started to buckle. "Looks like I get another helicopter ride tonight," he joked. Holding out his hand, Sierra reached for him but the blood made his fingers slippery. She forced a smile on her face as tears rolled down her cheeks. "Tell Joan, I'm not sorry. For anything." Max struggled to talk. "Make sure you tell her that."

"Don't forget about the baby," Bernice sniggered.

"Gwendolyn is a nightmare no one will remember," Sierra retorted.

"Not that baby. Tell her, *Max*, you tell her." She glared at Sierra, a triumphant snarl on her lips. "Talk fast, before it's a fatherless baby."

Sierra whirled around, looking at Max. "A baby? You and Joan?" Max shrugged and nodded weakly.

Bernice started screaming and pointing at Sierra. "She's stabbed him. She stabbed him." People from nearby tables started surging around her. Sierra could hear the shocked reactions and angry shouts.

Grabbing Sierra's neck, Bernice whispered harshly in her ear. "I guess you two aren't such good friends, after all." Her cackling set Sierra's nerves on fire.

The barmaid rushed over with towels. Sierra turned away, her mind numb, feeling helpless as Bernice disappeared in the crowd. She grabbed a towel and kept her hands on Max's wound trying to control the blood loss. Joan was pregnant? That explained the not drinking alcohol and the queasy stomach. But to not tell her? What was that all about?

Paramedics arrived and Bernice pushed deeper into the crowd, elbowing bystanders out of the way. Sierra slid over to the other chair. Where was Joan now? Had the police already found her? Maybe that was the 'disorganization' Bernice had talked about. And if Max is here - then where was Marcus and Charles Henry?

A paramedic bumped into Sierra as he pulled the gurney forward. The team was ready to load Max into an ambulance. "Where are we going?" Sierra started to follow them.

"Miss, you're staying with us."

Sierra turned to find two officers, one with his fists on his hips, looking at her sternly.

"I need to go with my friend. I didn't do this. It was Bernice, she stabbed him - and now she's getting away."

"So she's your accomplice? The waitress said you two came in together and shared a table."

Sierra groaned inwardly. "No, I'm not anybody's accomplice. I'm the victim. She kidnapped me. The only reason I didn't try to get away earlier was because if I did, she'd call *her* accomplice, who would then kill my friend."

"Your friend, Max?"

"No, my friend Joan. Max is her boyfriend. I don't know how he got to Whistler."

The officers looked skeptical, and Sierra felt a pounding headache coming on. "It's complicated," she said. The police merely stared at her, waiting. "Let me start at the beginning."

"Good idea," he said.

Half hour later, back at the Whistler RCMP station, and after Sierra handed them a photocopy of her passport that she'd kept folded in her purse. The constables checked out her passport, and Sierra was free to go. Max, in the meantime, had been taken by ambulance to the Whistler medical clinic. Worst-case scenario, they would transfer him to Vancouver.

Stepping out of the station, Sierra couldn't stop shivering. She'd given them a description of Bernice and Rupert and explained Gwendolyn as well as she could. Where was Marcus? Her stomach hurt with indecision. Had Bernice followed through already and called Gwendolyn? Would Gwendolyn really kill Joan? She wanted to use the phone at the police station, but she was afraid she'd be stuck in another interrogation. After all, there were conflicting witness reports to sort out.

No. She'd walk back to the hotel, use the phone at the concierge desk to try to reach Marcus, then rent a car and drive back to Vancouver. She didn't have a chance to ask Max any questions, and no one could tell her if he'd be okay, or not. In the meantime, Bernice had disappeared. So where was Joan? She rubbed her arms. Where was Gwendolyn?

~~~

Rupert pulled into Shoppers Drug Mart on Burrard street, honking the horn to clear a path through the pedestrians crowding the parking lot. The streets of downtown Vancouver glowed, filled with locals and tourists alike, everyone enjoying another perfect summer evening. Joan felt tired and achy. Her stomach felt queasy, and she'd give anything to have the courage to jump out of the car and run into the crowd. The only thing that stopped her was Gwendolyn's threat to make the call and tell Bernice to hurt Sierra if she acted up or tried to escape.

The crowds...Joan straightened up. Why were the sidewalks getting crowded? It was almost 9:00pm, the stores would be closing shortly. She glanced over at Gwendolyn, who appeared quite pleased with herself. She was smiling as she stared intently at her tablet.

"Hey," Joan said. "I'm confused. How am I supposed to 'rob' Tiffany's with so many people around? Rupert and Gwendolyn ignored her. She took a closer look at the items that Gwendolyn had tossed at her earlier. A red rubber clown nose and a pair of plastic vampire teeth. What was she supposed to do with them?
~~~

"Here." Gwendolyn tossed something blue and shiny at her. "Time to get ready."

Joan grimaced. Oh great. She shook the short curly mess of acrylic fiber; it was a blue hair wig that smelled faintly musty.

Gwendolyn glanced at her watch. "Put your party outfit on, it's time to blend in."

Joan did what she was told. Moments later, she found herself on the street with Rupert on one side and Gwendolyn, tablet in hand, on the other, power walking down the street towards Tiffany's.

At just before 9pm, Rupert pulled an air horn from his backpack. He looked over at Gwendolyn. She touched her tablet and nodded. He pulled the trigger. Joan groaned and covered her ears; the sound was loud, long and obnoxious. Gwendolyn pushed her forward, moving quickly through the growing crowd. Joan tripped, but there too many people to actually fall, she merely regained her balance.

The scene was wild, crazy, and fluid. People were laughing and dancing in the street. Others had air horns as well. Everything was getting louder and louder. It felt like...organized chaos. Joan suddenly realized what was happening. There'd be no stopping Gwendolyn at Tiffany's. The police would soon be overwhelmed with hundreds of people downtown. "How?" she could barely believe what she was seeing.

"Social media," Gwendolyn replied. She pushed Joan up against a glass door. They were in front of Tiffany's.

~~~

Inside Tiffany's & Co, lights shimmered on various stones and precious metals tucked safely inside locked glass cases. Kris, the store manager, was wiping down the front counters, yet again. A few minutes until closing time, and one young couple from Calgary were looking for a wedding ring set.

Tiffany's had a high-end clientele, and if they were spending that much money, they were welcome to take their time. At the moment, the couple on vacation from Calgary was busy deciding on an engagement ring and matching bands. The bride-to-be couldn't decide between a marquis setting, or the Emerald cut.
~~~

Each Diamond sized at four carats, and then there were the surrounding stones to consider, which easily added another half carat to the price.

Marcus had to bite his tongue. When he married Sierra, he gave her a dainty, yellow gold, ring with a half-carat solitaire, with four, one-tenth carat Diamonds surrounding it. It was all he could afford at the time.

They'd married very young and didn't have a lot of money for several years. It took a lot of hard work, blood, sweat, and tears to build up his computer software business. He peered into the case. Maybe he would get her something. He knew she'd be very surprised.

Kris walked over to Marcus, who stood by the display of Emeralds. "You know, if you're going to look like a real customer, you should be taking a closer look at these."

She was teasing, Marcus realized, but shook his head. "Thanks, but Sierra has all the Emeralds she'll ever need."

"How about Australian fire opals? Your wife strikes me as a woman who likes the rich flash of color." She pointed to a cabinet unit sitting in a corner with three rows of gems gleaming against white velvet. "Come on, you can at least look. If not to keep you from being nervous, then do it for me. I'm ready to jump out of my skin." She paused to look around the open floor and all the cases filled with gold and gems. "Are you and Charles Henry sure Gwendolyn is coming here tonight?"

Marcus nodded. "It seemed the logical choice."

"Then I'm glad we have a police officer here, just in case."

Suddenly air horns started wailing in the street right outside, along with loud yelling. The doorman ran inside, locking the heavy glass door behind him. He looked scared. "It's crazy out there!"

Marcus grabbed Kris and moved over to the front counters. He kept his eyes on the double glass entrance doors. The police officer rushed up to the windows at the front of the store, radio in hand. "It's some kind of event, don't know if it's protesters or what." He motioned to the young couple, now confused and scared, holding onto each other. "I've been called in to help with crowd control. You two," he pointed at the couple. "We're exiting through the back. Now."

He glanced at Marcus and Charles Henry, who'd been in the back office. "Are you coming? Apparently, there's three blocks in the downtown area teeming with clowns. Hundreds of people wearing blue wigs and red noses." He shook his head in disgust. "And those damn air horns."

Marcus and Charles Henry shook their heads. The cop hesitated a moment. "Good luck," he said. Kris guided the newly engaged couple to the rear exit. The policeman and the doorman followed. Kris came back up front a few minutes later. "This whole thing has to be Gwendolyn's doing. I've heard she has a large social media following. I'd love to know what she said to get so many people to participate."

Charles Henry merely sighed. "Now I know she'll be showing up."

"I'm sorry about Willow, Charles," Kris said. "She was a delightful woman. Strong, sweet, I know you'll miss her." Fingering the cloth in her hands, she opened her mouth to speak. Then stopped. She stood there for a few moments, hesitating, then came to a decision. Looking Charles in the eye, she asked, "Do you want to see your wedding band?"

"What? I don't have a wedding band." He looked confused.

Kris smiled gently at his look. "Willow designed one for you, and paid for it herself. Her gift to you." Reaching into a drawer behind her she pulled out a small dark blue velvet case. Inside sat a dark metallic ring, with four gems in a channel setting across the top. One small pearl, a half-carat amethyst, a half-carat Ceylon Blue Sapphire and a half-carat Emerald. The gemstones looked very masculine set in the dark metal.

Charles Henry was speechless. Carefully he pulled the ring from its velvet-lined box and slowly slipped it on his left-hand ring finger. It was a perfect fit. Tears welled in his eyes. "I haven't even had the chance to see her. We came straight here from the airport. I still can't believe she's really gone." Kris handed him a tissue. He nodded his thanks as he wiped his eyes. He turned to face the double glass doors. "So, what night did you meet Joan?"

Kris smiled at the memory. "Friday night. She and Sierra came it a little before 7pm. Joan was interested in the yellow Diamonds. Sierra seemed too nervous to talk to me at first; maybe she thought I'd put pressure on her to purchase something. Then once Willow got here, the three of them were thick as thieves. They were admiring Willow's Sapphire wedding bracelet and the ring she had made for you. Between the three of them, they finished off two bottles of champagne." Charles Henry could believe that. Joan loved champagne.

Marcus was pacing near the manager's desk. The plan was, if and when Gwendolyn arrived - and Charles Henry was positive she would - Marcus would strike up a conversation with her, hoping to distract her long enough for Charles Henry to get into position to contain her. Then Kris would call 911, and hopefully everything could end quietly.

He tried to point to a pair of earrings, but found his hands shaking. Was Sierra safe? He knew she could defend herself, but could she do so against a weapon? And where was this older sibling Rupert? Did he have Sierra? Or Joan? Why separate the two women? He allowed himself a quick smile; he knew the answer to that thought. Of course, they would be separated. It would be the only way Gwendolyn could succeed.

Charles Henry glanced up at the clocks. "This waiting is driving me crazy."

A sudden, persistent, thudding caught their attention. A clown had been shoved hard against the glass doors. The person's face mushed sideways into the glass. Another clown stood next to the first one, holding a printed sign up against the glass.

"You know what I want." Kris read it out loud. Taking a closer look at whom she thought was Gwendolyn, but half her face looked more like raw hamburger. "Gwendolyn?"

The clown held up another sign. "Bracelet. Now." Kris turned towards Charles Henry. "What do we do?" Charles Henry walked up to the door. He could see Joan trying hard not to cry. Gwendolyn tapped on the glass with a gun, then she jabbed it into Joan's ribs.

Marcus stood next to Charles Henry. "What's the plan?" The older man's hard gaze never left Gwendolyn's face. "Give me a couple sheets of blank paper and a marker." Kris walked briskly behind the counter. Marcus could hear her shuffling things around as she quickly gathered up what Charles Henry required.

"Marcus, I need your back." Marcus obliged, stepping closer. Charles Henry worked quickly. And then held up a sign of his own.

Marcus watched Gwendolyn read it and snarled. Her blue eyes flashed in anger, the sneer would have been more effective if both sides of her face could move. Marcus couldn't help but stare. The infamous Gwendolyn. She was beautiful and grotesque at the same time. But it wasn't her damaged face that looked ugly. It was the hatred that emanated from her whole body. And the way her hand on the gun pressing into Joan's ribs. Her eyes shifted and Marcus found himself caught in her gaze. It wasn't hard to read her lips. "Uh, Charles? I don't know what you wrote, but she wants us to let her in." He turned to his friend. "Or else she'll kill Joan."

Kris tossed the keys to Charles. "Are you sure you want to do this?" she asked.

Charles grimaced. "No. But at the moment, I don't have a choice." He turned back to Kris and Marcus. "Be ready for anything."

Gwendolyn pushed her way in using Joan as cover, as soon as the door was unlocked, keeping a tight grip on Joan's neck. The gun still pointed at Joan's head. "I'll be blunt. I want the--" A push from behind bumped into her shoulders, knocking her down, as a flow of people fell into the store behind her. Air horns were blasting, everyone was shouting.

A shot rang out, and one of the time zones clocks above Kris's head exploded. Gwendolyn had fired the weapon. The crowd started to scatter. Screaming filled the air as Marcus and Charles tried to reach Joan, but there were too many bodies. Kris pounded on the silent alarm button. Marcus tried to keep the crowd from storming into the store, while Charles Henry tried to reach Joan. It was several minutes before any police arrived. By then, Gwendolyn and Joan had vanished.

The police detained Marcus and Charles Henry for questioning. Frustrated, Marcus couldn't stop pacing. Charles Henry wasn't any happier and the police were taking their time with all the questions. The whereabouts of the weapon was a concern for the police - including how did Gwendolyn acquire it. Marcus and Charles both started talking at once, pointing to the front of the store trying to explain that Gwendolyn was getting away, taking a hostage with her.

"Did Willow own a gun?" One officer asked questions while the other took notes. They had gathered various items from the melee, including the signs Gwendolyn and C.H. had written.

Charles Henry could only shrug. "It's possible, it would have belonged to her husband. Gwendolyn had been hired to downsize Willow's household goods, so its quite likely she found it, and kept it."

Impatient and anxious, the two men finally finish their interviews. Promising to stay in the city for the next few days, Marcus and Charles Henry were allowed to leave.

"My wife is missing, Gwendolyn has kidnapped Joan, and they're telling *me* not to leave town?" Marcus was outraged and angry, but not at the police. It was Gwendolyn he wanted.

Kris stopped them as they tried to leave out the heavy double glass front doors, pointing out news media presence on the nearby streets. "You may want to leave out the back."

"Good idea," Charles said. "We can catch a taxi back to the hotel."

"Wait," Marcus grabbed Charles's arm. "I want to go to Willow's home. It's where everything started, and we need a clue as to where Gwendolyn took Joan."

Charles, his gray face etched with sadness, shook his head. "I don't want to go there, but I think you're right. Let's check in with Max first, and see if he found anything at Whistler."

~~~

Sierra signed the second car rental form with a flourish, standing at the Lodge's concierge desk. The same clerk was still on duty, and Sierra explained that she and her friend had gotten into
~~~

an argument, and were now leaving in separate vehicles. The clerk merely shrugged, offered her condolences and took Sierra's credit card. She was offered a driver for a nominal fee, but Sierra didn't want to wait. The staffer offered her an outside line. Sierra thought she'd misdialed. The second time, her call went straight to Marcus's voicemail. After the third attempt, she left a frustrated message. What was the point of carrying a cell phone if you weren't going to answer it?

Her car was brought around to her. She paused a moment, looking around. Whistler was beautiful; maybe she and Marcus could come here another time. She glanced back at the hotel, a quick trip to the Ladies Room was in order, before heading down the mountain.

Where to go once she arrived in Vancouver? The hotel in Vancouver was a choice, but that didn't make sense. With Max in the Whistler Medical Clinic; that meant Marcus might be in Vancouver. Had Charles Henry arrived yet? She shook her head as she got into the car. Why on earth did Max show up at Whistler alone? What was he thinking?

The more she thought about it, the more she realized driving to Willow's home made sense. Everything started there. She knew the address, so the car's GPS could guide her there.

Once in the car and on the road, anxiety started creeping in. Why didn't Marcus answer his cell phone? Would the police catch Bernice? The RCMP always 'get their man', they told her at the station – but this was a crazy woman. She didn't know much about Gwendolyn, other than she was beyond angry Willow 'stealing' Charles Henry.

"Bernice," Sierra said out loud, "your sister is one crazy bitch."

"I think you're right," Bernice answered, sitting up from the backseat of the sedan.

Chapter THIRTEEN

Sierra gasped, and swerved slightly into the other lane, and then swerved back. "What are you doing in my car?" Both hands gripping the steering wheel, she looked into the rearview mirror. Bernice sat there, calmly. "How did you get away from the police?"

"I don't think my sister appreciates anything I've ever done for her." Bernice looked sad, as her gaze followed the half-moon outside the window.

Sierra's mind raced. Should she keep her talking? Ask questions? What?

"Are we going to Willow's house?" Bernice sounded tired.

"Possibly," Sierra answered. "Do you still have that knife?"

"No, I dropped it in the creek."

"That's a good place for it. So...why did you stab Max?" Sierra hoped this wasn't a volatile question.

"He was too pushy, and he sounded so phony. He didn't really want to talk with me. And mostly because he's a baby too, like Gwendolyn."

"He's my friend, and he was trying to help me," Sierra said softly. "He knew I was in danger."

Bernice's head flew up. "Danger? Not from me. Baby isn't happy with you, but you're like me. Neither are the youngest sibling...and we both like dogs. Big dogs."

"That's true, you and I both like big dogs. And Baby doesn't like dogs." Sierra kept her voice low. If Bernice was back to liking her for liking dogs, this could be a good thing.

"No," Bernice shook her head, sighing, "She pretty much doesn't like anything or anybody but herself. She's always been that way. Mama knew she was the last child she could have, so Baby was special."

Sierra noticed a sign showing Vancouver in 92 kilometers, about an hour away. What should she do now? Was Bernice coming to her senses? Was she now willing to help her rescue Joan from Gwendolyn? She needed to keep her talking. "So, Bernice, what does your mother think about Gwendolyn's behavior? Isn't she concerned?"

Bernice didn't answer right away. And when she did, her voice was hushed. "Mama's dead. Passed away fifteen years ago, right after Baby came in third runner up in the Miss British Columbia pageant. She blamed Mama. Daddy took ill at the same time, but he survived. He now lives in assisted living."

"Your parents were sick at the same time?" Sierra glanced in the rearview mirror to see Bernice nod. "What happened? Was it the flu, Legionnaires, or something like that?"

"Rupert and I...have our suspicions." Bernice reached down and pulled a bottled water out of a paper bag. "That's pretty much why we let her have her way. The rest of our family back in Quebec doesn't believe us. So, we keep things to ourselves." She twisted off the cap with a snap.

The hairs on the back of Sierra's neck stood up. Holy crap. She was driving with a crazy person breathing down her neck. She rolled back her shoulders and swallowed hard. "Bernice, are you in this car because you want to hurt me?"

"What? No. I needed to get away from the police. I saw you by the car at the hotel when the gal gave you the keys. You ran back in, and there weren't any cops around, so I figured you'd be heading back to Vancouver. You left this car unlocked. I thought I'd hitch a ride. No need to stay here, and I wasn't going to wait to take the train tomorrow."

"Okay. I'm glad I could help." Sierra realized she should just drive and leave things be. But then, that wasn't her style. "You know, we could have left much earlier in the day if you'd just told me that's what you wanted to do. No one had to get hurt, especially Max."

"I know. But I didn't talk to Rupert until after we both left that pub. He said it would be a good idea to meet him."

Sierra's hands were sweaty. She'd never had sweaty hands before. She'd been afraid, and nervous, but this was something new. Now what? Originally, she thought Bernice to be harmless, until she stabbed Max. And, she was Gwendolyn's twin. What chance did she have once Rupert was in the picture? The highway was dark, with few cars. She suddenly swerved into the other lane and then swerved back. Bernice fell against the car door, hitting her head on the passenger window.

"Hey!" Bernice rubbed the crown of her head. "What was that for?"

"Sorry," Sierra lied. "Thought I saw a bear in the road."

Bernice was quiet in the backseat, still rubbing her head. The conversation at a lull for the moment, Sierra frantically thought about what to do next. For a crazy moment the story of the frog and the scorpion flashed through her mind. And she knew she was the frog. "I can do this," she whispered to herself. "I can do this."

"Don't worry, Bernice," Sierra said out loud, hoping her voice didn't quaver. She deepened her voice to boost her confidence. "I have a plan."

Bernice slid across the back seat until she was directly behind Sierra. "I have a plan too," her fingertips softly rubbing the back of Sierra's neck. "I'll give you directions once we're closer to town." Frustrated, her stomach clenched at Bernice's touch, her eyes filling with tears. Oh damn, sorry Marcus. Here we go again.

~~~

The house was dark when Marcus and Charles Henry were dropped off out in front. Marcus paid the driver. "Is there a garage on this property?" Marcus asked Charles Henry as the taxi drove away.

"There was at one time, it's in the back, with access off a side street. Willow turned it into a yoga studio about ten years ago. It's a small studio, and she loved it. That's where I first met her." Charles Henry's eyes glistened. He cleared his throat and searched through his pockets. "I have house keys. I still can't believe she's not here anymore." Charles Henry led the way through the side gate and towards the back door of the kitchen. "She absolutely loved this garden. She lived here for thirty years. And she was
~~~

willing to leave it." He spread his arms to include the house and studio. "All of this, to live with me. It feels so empty, as if all her energy left this place when she did."

Stepping into the kitchen, he stopped suddenly. The house was empty, literally. Everything was gone. The furniture, the lamps, the rugs, all the kitchen supplies. Marcus found a light switch. The harsh glare showed empty walls, devoid of all artwork. Faint lines on the walls left shadows of where the china hutch had been. There were fresh scratch marks on the hardwood floors; evidence of careless, movers dragging out bigger pieces of furniture.

Charles Henry was speechless. He stared at all the emptiness. His mouth opened, but he had no words. Marcus watched the incredulous horror grow on his face. This was not what Willow's fiancé expected to see.

"Must have been a big turnout for the estate sale this weekend," Marcus offered. "You know, to raise cash, since you two were moving to Australia. So maybe, this means, it was really successful?"

Charles Henry didn't answer. Instead, he raced up the stairs, and headed for the bedrooms. Marcus waited in the empty living room while staring through the dining room, and the dining room windows where he had a clear view to the back yard. The house was spacious, easily over twenty-five hundred square feet. He could hear Charles Henry moving from room to room upstairs. Walking into the dining room, Marcus looked intently into the backyard. There were strange glowing lights near the yoga studio. As he watched, the number of lights grew. What was going on?

"There's something wrong." Charles Henry found Marcus staring out the back windows. "Everything is gone. Everything. Her suitcases, my quilt." He shook his head, confused and frustrated, he turned to follow Marcus's gaze outside. "What the hell?" He charged for the kitchen door and threw it open. A moment later he disappeared, swallowed by the darkness. Marcus followed, wishing he had a weapon.

Marcus could only hope he didn't trip over any little fences, step on any garden gnomes, or worse, end up face-first in a fish pond. He caught up with Charles Henry in near pitch-blackness, as they skirted up to a small round glass table. At the moment the table was covered with lit candles. And the shapes of several women standing nearby became visible.

"Charles Henry?" One of the women stepped forward. "Charles?"

"Yes," he answered. He stood still and waited.

"I'm Amelia, a friend of Willow's. I'm aware we're technically trespassing. But we wanted to honor Willow's spirit and her friendship. Is this okay?" Amelia's soft voice sounded doubtful while asking her question. "Her real estate manager and her mother, both told us to 'piss off'. But considering how Willow died, we figured she needed us." Amelia came up to Charles Henry and hugged him. "You need us."

His eyes adjusting to the candlelight, Marcus counted seven women standing in a circle in the garden. Joan and Sierra were not with them. Damn it. "Have you ladies been in the house? Have you seen anyone enter the house late this afternoon, or tonight?"

"Rupert was here earlier this evening. He had three other guys with him, helping him move out the dining room table and china cupboard."

"And the bed sets," another woman spoke up. "With the mattresses, too."

"We couldn't believe it when her mother threw away Willow's suitcases," added another woman. "Didn't even bother to see if there was anything important in them."

"We saved the suitcases," Amelia added bitterly. "We hoped we would see you. And here you are." She hugged Charles Henry again. "She loved you so much."

"So," Marcus asked. "You ladies have held a candlelight vigil for the last two nights?" They all nodded.

"Thank you, all of you," Charles Henry said; he extracted himself from Amelia's hug. "Willow loved all of you as well. It was very hard for her to leave her friends."

Amelia smiled through her tears. "Not as hard as you think, Charles. She was very much looking forward to her next life adventure, with you."

Using a flashlight now, two of the ladies rolled up several pieces of luggage onto the grass next to Charles Henry. Two large pieces, and one carry-on. Marcus went to lift them. They were not light. "I'll go put these in the yoga studio, so you can look through them later, okay?" Charles Henry merely nodded.

One of the ladies turned on her flashlight and grabbed the handle of the carry-on. "I'll roll this one for you."

Marcus nodded his thanks and motioned to the woman. "Lead on." Once on the gravel path, it was easy to find the studio. Marcus looked up the street at an oncoming car and watched it park in front of the house. He grabbed the woman and pulled her quickly behind the studio. "We have company. Go tell the ladies the candlelight vigil is over. All of you need to leave. Now."

"Hold on now," she began protesting, "you can't tell us what to do."

Marcus grabbed her arm and frog-stepped her back to the others. "Listen to me. Willow's death was not an accident. There is a very dangerous person I need to deal with, and I want all of you ladies out of the way."

"Gwendolyn," the woman said. "We're well aware she's more than a little obsessed with Charles Henry. Did she kill Willow?"

Marcus sighed, there wasn't time for explanations. "Not sure, but I think so. Please, for your safety, put out your candles, and leave."

The women were talking quietly, while Marcus grabbed Charles Henry's arm. "Someone's here. It could be Gwendolyn with Joan, or it could be Sierra. Or even this Rupert guy, no clue. But we need to have a plan."

"We need to call the police," Charles Henry said.

"Agreed, but I want to see who's in the house first. It's someone who doesn't want to be seen."

"How do you know this?" Charles Henry asked.

"Because they've turned off the lights in the kitchen," answered Marcus. He turned toward Amelia. "Hey, we need your flashlights, please," he added, seeing Amelia's hard look.

Irritated, Amelia handed over the lights. "We can help, you know."

"Fine. You can call the police, and report an intruder. And make sure you tell them it's not us." He caught movement of one of the women holding their phone. He pointed to the road. "Don't forget, call the police after you and your friends leave the property... now."

Marcus and Charles Henry stared at the kitchen door. "Better safe than sorry," Marcus said. "Is there anything in the yoga studio we could use for a weapon?"

Charles Henry shook his head. "There's yoga mats and disinfectant wipes..." he snapped his fingers. "And several sets of hand weights, from 2 pounds up to 10." He paused as he glanced at the darkened house. "Unless they've sold all that stuff, too."

"That's good. Not too lethal, yet useful enough to slow someone down if we hit them just right." Marcus handed over a flashlight. "Let's go find out."

Plans made, the men made their way in the dark past the bushes and to the studio. Charles Henry used another key.

Chapter FOURTEEN

"You're a terrible driver."

Bernice's comment brought a smile to Sierra's lips. "Everybody seems to think that, I don't understand why."

Sierra had parked a little further down the street from the house, watching in dark silence as the last car full of Willow's friends drove away.

Sierra was sure she'd spotted Marcus, causing adrenaline to shoot through her veins like an electric jolt; her fingers itched to hit the horn, or flash the car lights, anything to catch his attention. But she didn't dare move. Bernice was fast, and Sierra didn't trust her. The house appeared quiet. Both of them could see where lights upstairs had been left on.

"Looks like Rupert's crew didn't turn off all the lights," Bernice said.

"You don't think Willow's mother, or other family members could be inside?"

"No." Bernice shook her head. "Willow and her mother were estranged."

"That's a shame. Life's too short for fighting within families."

"Your family never fights?" Bernice sounded incredulous. "Not even your siblings?"

"I didn't say that. But we always talk it out. We don't hold grudges, or shun each other."

Bernice merely shrugged. "I think I've always been the 'black sheep' of the family. Me or Rupert."

"That sounds sad," Sierra replied.

"You get used to it."

"How many siblings do you have?" Sierra hadn't seen a knife during the ride down the mountain, but that didn't mean there wasn't one.

"I have four older brothers, Rupert is the youngest of them, then me and Gwendolyn."

"Oh, you're fraternal twins then?"

Bernice nodded.

"That's got to suck," Sierra said, "you missed out being the baby of the family by just a few minutes?"

"Oui, that is true." Bernice pushed Sierra towards the car door. "No more talk. Let's go inside." She quickly slid out of the back seat of the car as Sierra opened the driver side door.

Rats, Sierra thought, no chance to lock Bernice in the car. It wouldn't have lasted long, but she could have run in between some of the houses or yards and escaped. "What if Gwendolyn is already here?"

Bernice pursed her lips. "I guess the lights mean your friend is here, too."

"Now what?" Sierra asked.

The only response was another shrug. Sierra slammed the car door hard. "You know your sister is crazy. What is your plan? Are you ready to be an accomplice to murder? When do you get to live your life, for yourself, Bernice? When?"

Bernice clapped her hands over her ears. "Enough!"

Sierra rushed at her, grabbing at her neck and pulling the woman's jacket off her shoulders, catching her hands in the sleeves. Sierra tugged, pulling the sleeves all the way off. A knife clattered onto the road. Sierra grabbed it before Bernice could.

Holding the knife, she watched Bernice start to cry. "Oh for Heaven's sakes." Sierra not-so-gently pushed Bernice toward the house and up the front steps. "You're a damn liar. You said you didn't have a knife." She'd felt sorry for her, but after seeing her stab Max, she didn't trust her for a second. She pulled Bernice's cell phone and house key out of a jacket pocket.

She hesitated before pushing open the door and decided to shove Bernice in first - just in case. If the house really was empty, then she'd turn off all the lights - and call Marcus. They stood still in the foyer, listening for voices. Nothing. "Hello?" Sierra called out. Still nothing, and worse, the house sounded empty.

The house was empty. Every stick of furniture was gone. No rugs, no lamps, nothing. Sierra and Bernice walked towards the dining room. "Turn off the kitchen lights, Bernice." Standing in the darkness Sierra felt sick, all of Willow's possessions were gone. It was if someone wanted to wipe out her existence.

"Wow," Sierra said, "you guys weren't kidding when you said this place would be cleared out. I can't believe everything sold in just two days. Where do you take the left over stuff?"

"Our company has a warehouse in each province," Bernice replied. "We buy what's left over for pennies on the dollar, and then we sell it."

"What about the personal items, like clothing?"

"The nicer things we sell, the rest we donate."

They were walking slowly past the row of kitchen windows that looked out over the backyard. Sierra could see a light shining at a neighbor's garage door. Sierra stopped "Hmm." That looked like a good idea. Her hand found the wall switches. There were two close together, and a third one all by itself. She flipped that switch. Bright light flooded the back steps and into the yard.

"Okay," Sierra said. "This will let us see anyone coming." She waggled the cell phone at Bernice. "And now, I'm calling Marcus." She pressed a button. Nothing. And again. Nothing. The phone was dead.

~~~

"Damn him!"

Joan watched Gwendolyn's temper explode from her side of the car. She'd pressed herself further against the passenger door. Gwendolyn's plans were falling apart. Rupert had disappeared after the Tiffany's debacle. She was forced to listen as the former beauty queen called him everything awful, then switched to French.

Joan flinched, but managed to stay quiet when Gwendolyn threw the cell phone at the car dashboard, followed by her blue hair wig and red nose. The cell phone just inches away, almost
~~~

within grabbing distance. Almost. But then again, this lady could totally lose her cool and shoot Joan out of pure frustration. Or aim the rental car into a traffic pole.

Just how out of control was she? Joan could still hear muttering in French. And she understood enough to know that if Rupert were smart - he'd stay gone. Joan couldn't blame the man; it wasn't nice of Gwendolyn to zap him with her Taser, just to check the voltage, as Rupert was unlocking the car. Joan quickly swallowed a nervous giggle.

Gwendolyn had laughed as Rupert crashed against the car hood and then slowly slid to the ground, wetting himself in the process. He'd thrown the car keys at her face; along with a few swear words of his own, as he staggered away into the crowd. Now trapped, Joan was riding from downtown and through different neighborhoods, heading back to Willow's house. Unable to move, she found herself paralyzed with fear. Despite the warm summer air, Joan suddenly felt very cold. Was her time running out?

The back porch light suddenly flashed on as Marcus and Charles Henry started their approach to the back of the house. They found themselves ducking for cover. "Well, that's that," Marcus said, picking himself up off the gravel walkway. The entire yard nearest the house was awash in bright white light. Their plan of sneaking into the house had failed before it even started.

Marcus looked over at Charles Henry and did a double take. The man was smiling. "What the heck?" And now the man was on the move. "Hey, wait for me," he called out softly. He could recognize a man on a mission. Charles stopped once he reached the far side of the house where the yard abutted an alley.

"This is a better way." Charles Henry knelt over a weathered barn door lying on the ground, held shut with a padlock.

"How? It's just a shed," Marcus was willing. But how would a shed help them find Sierra and Joan?

"It's the access to the old root cellar." Charles Henry said. He pulled out his key ring and fumbled for the smallest key.

"So?" Marcus couldn't figure it out. They were wasting precious time.

"It's another way into the house," Charles Henry said, with a quick twist of his wrist, the lock released. He then pulled at the old weathered boards, throwing them back on their hinges. "A mud room connects to *this* root cellar." He grinned and started climbing down dingy, rickety wooden stairs.

"Looks more like a tornado shelter," Marcus said, following right behind him. No way he was staying behind. But he started to change his mind as he pulled at old, clingy spider webs and coughing as disturbed dust tickled his nose.

Short steps brought the two men at the bottom of the staircase. Marcus turned on his flashlight. No sign of a door. The staircase stopped at a wall. "Are you sure it's still here?"

"Oh yes," Charles Henry pointed to the far corner. "Willow stored some boxes down here."

"She carried them down these stairs?" Marcus found that hard to believe, what with all the spider webs and dust.

"No, no, not from here. This is the original cold room, and..." he paused to wipe his hands on his shirt. "Ah, here's the door." With a steady push he could only move it a few inches.

"It's stuck?" Marcus handed over his flashlight. Charles Henry grabbed it and held it at the gap of the opened door. The light caught the edge of folded cardboard boxes shoved up against it from the other side. A couple had fallen on the floor, just under the door, blocking it from opening. The flashlight slipped from Charles's grasp, landing with a dull onto the dirt floor.

"Wait," Marcus said. "I saw something." Picking up the flashlight he pointed the beam towards the near wall, illuminating rows of old glass jars of pickles on dusty wood planked shelves...and several new small boxes.

Charles Henry reached for the boxes and cursed under his breath. "These belonged to Willow, she would never had sold them or given them away." He lifted a pair of earrings out of a dark blue velvet box. The Blue Sapphires and surrounding white Diamonds sparkled under the light still held by Marcus. "These...these were my engagement present to Willow. After she said yes, she never took them off. Never. One of them...look, the back has been broken off. Something happened." The anguish etched on his face, hardened. "Someone hid these here. And my money's on Gwendolyn."

"I'm sorry, Charles Henry." Marcus couldn't think of anything else to say.

~~~

Sierra threw the useless cellphone into the stainless steel sink. Bernice's laughter fueled her frustration. With nothing else to throw, she began opening and slamming kitchen cupboard doors. Anything to drown out the wild laughter. Still fuming, knife in hand, Sierra leaned forward until she was nose to nose with Bernice. "So, no cellphone. How do you know we're supposed to be here? What if Gwendolyn is trying to call you?"

Bernice's smile dropped to a smirk, and she shrugged. Still, a frown creased her brow as she leaned over the sink and stared out into the backyard.

"With no phone," Sierra continued, "Rupert can't reach you either."

"We'll have to wait here." Pouting now, Bernice drew herself up to her full height of five foot seven, her arms folded defiantly.

"You can wait alone, as far as I'm concerned," Sierra said. "No more games, I'm going to find Marcus." It had to be him that she saw by the yoga studio, it had to be. She didn't know how much longer she could stay brave on her own.

"If you leave..." Bernice started.

"Yeah, yeah, Joan's no longer safe." Sierra held up the knife she'd taken from Bernice. "You know what? Since you're a liar, I don't believe you." The house was dark, but not for long. Sierra had changed her mind, deciding she needed to flip every light switch she could touch. "I'd tie you up, but this place is stripped to the walls. Rupert really cleaned this place out."

The bright back porch light glowed onto the hardwood floors of the kitchen and the dining room like a full moon. Sierra spotted a downstairs bathroom. "I'm adding more light to the situation." She flipped a nearby light switch. Only the kitchen went bright, the chandelier that had hung over the dining room table was gone.
~~~

Stepping toward the front door through the living room, Sierra's feet stopped at the bottom of the staircase. Her heart ached. She couldn't suppress a shiver as she imagined Willow's broken body lying there on the floor, when just a few days before, she'd been full of life and deeply in love. Ready for a new adventure.

"It could already be too late, for Joan."

Sierra jumped. Bernice stood just behind her, the woman's breath tickling the hair on the back of her neck. Cringing, Sierra swung around and pushed Bernice up against a wall. "Enough!" Sierra spat, between clenched teeth. "I've had all I can take from you."

Bernice grinned, and even with her face in the shadows, Sierra could see the crazy in her eyes. "Bernie, you are as nuts as your sister." Bernice squirmed free from Sierra. "Oh, no, you don't."

The woman giggled and ran down the dark hallway. Sierra chased after her, flipping on light switches wherever her fingers could find them. A bathroom blazed in cream and peach, while further down the hall, an empty bedroom with soothing sage colored walls, dark wood floors and bare closets, but Bernice was not hiding in there.

Sierra shoved a swinging hall closet door closed, and continued to the last room in the hallway. The door was closed. No lights showed from under the door, Sierra skidded to a stop. She struggled to control her breathing while carefully listening. Was Bernice behind the door? Did she lock the door and escape out the window? Indecision gripped her. Should she rush in? Or should she backtrack and run out the front, hopefully catching her in the yard?

"Every second counts. Every second counts," Sierra murmured. Tears welled in her eyes. What was the right thing to do? She'd turned to backtrack down the hallway when a scuffling sound caught her attention. Stopping for the briefest of seconds, Sierra shifted her weight and threw herself against the door.

~~~
~~~

With the door wedged open a few inches, Marcus could barely see inside the room, the sudden light in the room helped, but the big desk still blocked the door. He could hear movement in the next room. Someone was struggling to shove the desk across a thick carpet. He motioned Charles Henry to stand ready. "We're going in," he said grimly.

Charles Henry shoved the jewelry into his pocket and grabbed a dirty shelf board from the floor. It was the length of a baseball bat. He held it like one, too. "Ready."

Taking a deep breath, and using his body weight, Marcus shoved the small door open. He tumbled through the small entry way and onto the carpet, knocking down a woman. She stared up at him; her eyes and lips round with fear.

"Who the hell are you?" Marcus barked, just as surprised as she was, but no way would he let her know that.

"Who the hell are *you*?" Angry and scared, Bernice scrambled to her feet, and stood in a ready, fighting stance. "Don't mess with me, I've got a knife."

Marcus glared at her as he slowly got to his feet. Before he could reply, Charles Henry stuck his head out of the small door, glancing around the room.

At that moment, Sierra catapulted through the door from the hallway and into the room. She lost her balance and fell, but quickly rolled onto her hands and knees, grabbing frantically at Bernice's ankles. "Don't let her go!" she yelled. "She stabbed Max."

Marcus blocked Bernice as she struggled to climb onto the desk and crawl out the now open window. Charles Henry grabbed an arm and tightened his grip on the woman as she tried to kick him. "I know you," he said. Bernice stopped struggling. "I know you, you're Gwendolyn's sister." She leaned against the desk, her hair hanging in her face. "Bernice, you don't have to protect her anymore." Charles Henry loosened his grip and tried to pat her on the back. She slapped his hand away.

Shaking her head, she tried to blink away the tears. "You don't understand. I don't have a choice." Shrugging her shoulder, she shoved her hands in her jeans pocket and pulled out a box cutter. The sharp tip caught everyone's attention.

"There's nowhere to run," Charles Henry said.

"She'll blame this on me," Bernice said. "I'll have to take the blame." She held the knife tip tightly against her throat. "I didn't kill Willow. Honest - she was kind and loving. I liked working with her."

Charles Henry nodded. "I believe you, Bernice. Willow liked you too, she told me so."

"What about your dogs?" Sierra swallowed hard. "If you hurt yourself, who'll take care of your pets?"

A half laugh, half sob escaped Bernice's lips. "What does it matter? Who will take care of them while I'm in prison?" She pushed the knife tip against her throat, a small line of blood welled against her pale skin.

"I will," Sierra said. Marcus rolled his eyes, but said nothing. "I believe that you didn't kill Willow. But you did stab Max."

The sound of the front door slamming into a wall caught everyone's attention. Sierra gasped. "Is that Joan?"

"No," Bernice shook her head, her hands trembling, as the knifepoint creased another, deeper, streak of blood across her throat. Blood trickled down faster, staining her shirt. "It's Gwendolyn."

Charles Henry started toward the door. Bernice pushed Sierra into Marcus and they fell, tangled, against the wall, allowing her time to scramble onto the desk and out the open window. Sierra and Marcus could only stare out into the darkness. "Okay," Marcus said, "she's a lot faster than she looks."

"Never mind," Charles Henry said. "Gwendolyn is dangerous. Let me go talk to her. Once Joan is safely out of harm's way..." His eyes met Marcus's. "I need you to take the girls out the back way." The door closed and he was gone.

Sierra turned to her husband. "What girls? Does he mean Joan and me? Seriously?" Before he could respond, she peppered him with more questions. "Is that Charles Henry? How long have you been in Vancouver? Did you get my messages?"

Marcus pulled her close and kissed her. Sierra wrapped her arms around him and kissed him back. "I'm glad to see you, too." She stifled a yawn. "I am so tired."

"Me, too." Marcus said. "But the night's not over yet."

~~~

"So, Charles Henry," Gwendolyn held her chin high, keeping her hands in her jacket pocket.

"Where's Joan?" Charles walked over to the bottom of the stairs.

"Oh, she's a little tied up at the moment, but she's fine." Her eyes narrowed. "For now."

"What is all this about, Gwendolyn?"

"How can you ask that?" She pulled out the gun. Her hands trembled. "It's all about you and me."

"And Willow," Charles added, nodding to the stairs. "I found your hiding place." He opened his hands, the glint of Sapphire and white Diamond earrings filled the room. "I know what you did. And if it takes the rest of my life...I will bring you to justice." He stood there, all anger drained out of his body. All he had left was grief, and pity.

Gwendolyn licked her lips as she stared at the gems. "What about justice for me?" Her anger swelled, overloading every pore of her body until all she could see were the jewels, hazed in red. "Where's the love of my life for me? You?" She scoffed, contempt frothing from her lips. "What a fool you are. I should have known, I should have paid closer attention to the clues, you're not worthy of me."

Her words were coming faster now, and louder. "I tried to help you better yourself, worthy of standing beside me. I ignored your weakness, believing you could learn from me." Her voice was hoarse from shouting. "You truly are a disappointment." She held the gun with both hands now, pointing it at his head.

The front door flung open. This time it was Rupert, arriving in a flourish. "Hold up, Baby," he said, waving his hands at her. He held up the red deposit bag. Gwendolyn didn't take notice, she kept her eyes off Charles Henry.
~~~

"Rupert," she said crossly, "Where have you been? You imbecile - everything has gone wrong and it's all your fault."

Rupert moved closer, standing behind her. "The family is demanding you return to Quebec."

"Ridiculous. This estate sale isn't closed yet." Her arms were growing tired, she lowered the gun to her side, still pointed it at Charles Henry. "Where's Bernice? And where's...your cousin's little buddy?" Gwendolyn's eyes never left Charles Henry's face. She enjoyed the power she held over the man, simply by pointing a weapon.

She'd accidently fired it in the jewelry store, and had found it intoxicating. Such power in her hands, the carnage she could cause at her fingertips. Her usual arsenal merely included cutting words. She could slash a person's ego into shreds with ease. But a gun...to fire a weapon was so much more satisfying.

Her strong personality had always gotten her whatever she wanted. That, plus her position and status within the family. She smiled at her former lover. "So, we're at an impasse, why don't you have a seat?" she nodded towards the stairs. "Unless you're ready to hand over those earrings?"

Charles Henry didn't move. "When you admit you killed Willow, I will give you the earrings." His hands shifted to give her a better view of the glittering stones. "Just tell me the truth, and they're yours."

Rupert moved closer, but still behind Gwendolyn's aim. "We must hurry. You don't understand. They're demanding you appear. They want you in Quebec tomorrow." He struggled to keep his voice steady, but urgency vibrated with every word. "We must leave. Now."

Indecision creased Gwendolyn's face. Damn the family. They were always in her way. The burning sensation on her face was becoming unbearable, despite the earlier medical attention. But now...perhaps it was time to retreat and recuperate. And then she'd crush Charles Henry and his rude, obnoxious cousin. That woman. She deserved a bullet to the face - not to kill her, no, just to leave her disfigured. She deserved to know what that felt like.

"Gwendolyn." Rupert broke her train of thought. "Let's go. Now. We'll use the cousin's rental car, that'll add a hefty fee to her bill, yes?"

"You're right, Rupert." She kept the gun pointed at Charles Henry. "It's time to leave." She stared longingly at the gems in his hand. "Hang on to those for me. I'll be back for them - and your cousin." She pulled the car keys from her pocket and tossed them to Rupert.

Then she pulled a piece of quilted fabric from her pocket and started wiping down the gun, watching Charles's eyes narrow as he recognized the fabric. "We mustn't be messy," she said, smirking at this man who had broken her heart. Her whole face felt inflamed now. She handed the gun over to Rupert. "Let's go."

Rupert eyed the tall, quiet man, still standing by the stairs, one hand on the banister. "I released your cousin," he said. "She's heading for the back door. I'm sorry for your loss-"

"Don't speak to him." Angrily, Gwendolyn shoved Rupert towards the door.

"You're not going to succeed." Charles Henry said, his voice hushed and cold. "You will be caught and punished."

"Oh really? Is your precious, dead, Willow going to stop me?" Laughing, she walked out the front door being held open by Rupert.

Bright lights flashed in her face, blinding Gwendolyn. She couldn't see, but she could tell the front porch and the yard were full of people. A microphone was shoved in her face. "Is it true you're responsible for the Indie Video Contest that's been causing so much chaos in downtown Vancouver?"

"What?" Gwendolyn held her hands over her eyes.

"Did you know you're being called the mastermind of the shock and awe Indie Video contest?"

Gwendolyn turned away from the voice, only to find yet another microphone shoved at her. "Ms. Symms, what do you think about the charges about to be filed against you by the RCMP for vandalism, and inciting riots in the downtown, including Stanley Park?"

"What?" She couldn't see her way through the crowd.

"Do you think its fair that you will be held responsible for all the unnecessary 911 emergency calls for the past three days?"

"Is it true, Ms. Symms, that your company, Royalty Estate Sales, is going to pay the one million dollar prize offered in the contest?"

"Are you, Ms. Symms, judging the contest yourself, or do you have staff for that?"

"Leave me alone." Overwhelmed by all the questions, blinded by the constant camera flashes, Gwendolyn called out to Rupert, but he didn't answer. He wasn't there.

“Ms. Symms, is it true you're going in for plastic surgery for your injured face?”

She found herself standing on the front porch alone, except for a swarm of TV crews and reporters that surrounded her. Hands covering her face, she stepped back until she backed up against the front door. She turned away from the crowd, desperate to find the door handle.

"Ms. Symms, is it true you created this contest as part of a plot, to distract police while attempting to rob Tiffany's?"

Sobbing now, Gwendolyn finally felt the door handle and pushed hard, anxious to get away. The door was locked. “Leave me alone!” Desperate to get away from the media she jumped off the porch and ran around the side of the house. The media surged forward. They weren't going to let their subject disappear.

Across the street, Marcus, Sierra, Joan, and Charles Henry watched the reporters. Amelia silently approached Charles, motioning him over to her. She went and stood by a policeman. They talked quietly for a minute, then she pulled out a tablet and a flash drive.

Together, they stared at the small screen. Amelia had set the video so it showed an empty staircase for about five seconds. Then a woman's body, Willow's body, rolled violently, awkwardly, down the stairs, landing hard - face first on the marble time floor. A pool of blood growing underneath her. Amelia started to cry, her body shaking with sobs. Charles Henry kept his eyes on the video.

It showed Amelia immediately following Willow down the stairs, crying, her movements agitated. Charles Henry could see her speaking as she knelt down and tried to revive the unconscious woman at the bottom of the stairs. She then ran out of the room and the range of the camera. The next person to come into camera range was Gwendolyn, as she entered through the front door. It was clear she was shocked seeing Willow's body at the bottom of the stairs.

But instead of rushing to help, she stepped over Willow's body and roughly pulled the Sapphire and Diamond earrings off Willow's earlobes. She then placed her foot on Willow's neck and pressed down, quick and hard. After that, Willow lay still, and Gwendolyn is seen pocketing the earrings, walking towards the hallway - a smirk on her face.

Charles Henry turned the video off and pocketed the flash drive, handing the tablet back to Amelia. He then pulled her into his arms and hugged her, and for several moments they grieved, together. Charles kissed her wet, tear-stained cheeks. "Thank you," he whispered. "This will bring justice for our Willow." Amelia nodded. She turned and walked with the policeman across the street where other officers were waiting.

He walked back towards the others who were waiting by the car. "I think Rupert was going to use this flash drive to blackmail Gwendolyn. But instead, he'd had enough of her threats and poor treatment and gave Amelia this copy. Turns out he made several copies, including one for the police."

Joan was sobbing now, hugging her cousin. "What were you looking at?"

Charles Henry shook his head. "Evidence - that will condemn Gwendolyn. And bring justice for Willow."

"I want to see it," Joan said. Her wrists were still sore from the handcuffs Gwendolyn had slapped on her. Rupert had released her from the trunk, telling her to wait for her friends.

"Me, too," chimed Sierra. She was still pulling bits of spider web off her sweater after Marcus had guided her through the old cellar. A secret exit...she loved it. They were leaning against Joan's rental car. Marcus and Sierra had spotted Joan, angry and still, freshly released from the trunk of the car, and they found the keys in an envelope tucked under a windshield wiper.

Charles Henry had run out back through the kitchen, along with Rupert, who quickly disappeared in the dark. Willow's yoga friends stood in the front yard, their candles creating a warm yellow glow across the front lawn. Reporters were interviewing them.

Charles Henry, his eyes bright with tears, shook his head. "No. I want you to remember her as you met her that first night. Full of life. And happy."

Joan reached out and hugged her cousin. "Oh, Charles, I'm so sorry." They turned to watch what had turned into a media circus. More news crews arrived, followed by two more police vehicles.

"Well," Sierra said. "Looks like Gwendolyn has all the attention she ever wanted." She looked over at Marcus. "Have you spoken to Max? Is he okay?"

Marcus nodded. "He'll be fine. The knife missed anything major. He'll be sore for a few weeks. Probably need some physical therapy too."

"What?" Joan, who was leaning on Charles Henry, jerked her head up. "Max? He's here? What happened? What knife? Take me to him, now!"

"Really?" Sierra asked. "You've been mad at him for days. Is there anything you want to tell us?"

"No," Joan was squirming under everybody's gaze, especially her cousin's.

"Huh. So why does Bernice think you're pregnant?"

Joan opened her mouth, but no words came out. "I...I..." she stammered. "I don't know why she'd say that."

Sierra pursed her lips. "Huh. So, how come *I* think you're pregnant? I've been watching you. You've been queasy, vomiting, not drinking any alcohol - and mad at Max because - and you told me this - he broke an important promise."

Arms folded, Joan pouted. "Fine. I *might* be pregnant. I don't know for sure yet."

Charles Henry hugged her. "I suggest we go visit Max, and while we're there, let's find out."

~~~

"What the hell were you thinking?"

Despite the closed door, Joan's voice could easily be heard in the hallway where Sierra, Marcus, and Charles Henry were leaning against the far wall waiting.

"Do you think she's upset because he was trying to rescue her and Sierra?" Marcus asked.

Sierra shook her head no. As did Charles Henry.

"Why not?"

"I have a feeling its more personal than that," Charles Henry said. Marcus's bewildered look made him shrug. "That's just how my cousin thinks."

Marcus pushed off the wall. "I'm going for coffee from somewhere other than the hospital cafeteria." He grabbed Sierra at her waist and pulled her to him, kissing her deeply. "I'll pick up some scones, too." She smiled as he lumbered down the hall and out the nearest exit, anxious to escape.

Despite the occasional raised voices, Sierra figured for the most part things were calming down. "So, Rupert and Bernice apparently have vanished. Do you think they'll ever be found and charged with anything?"

Charles Henry shook his head. "Who knows? Gwendolyn was humiliated on TV and I presume is now in jail. We'll have to wait and see what happens."

Sierra nodded. She looked at the closed door down the hall. "Do you think its safe to go in yet?"

Charles Henry glanced at his watch. "Hard to say. Let's give them another five minutes."

Fidgeting, Sierra lasted thirty seconds. She walked over to the door and rapped on it sharply. "Wrap it up in there, you two. I'm hungry."

The door opened, and Joan stuck her head out. "C'mon in." She looked tired, and tear stains streaked her cheeks. Max was
~~~

sitting up, a goofy grin on his face. He looked pale and drawn but appeared to be in good spirits.

"Max," Sierra said as she reached his bedside. "You are a complete dumb ass. What possessed you to approach me and Bernice at that bar?"

His smile dimmed as he shook his head. "Huh. A 'thank you' would be nice. I didn't know she'd have a weapon, much less *stab* me with it. She didn't look like a killer." He shot her a look. "At least I gave you a chance to get away."

Sierra turned toward Joan, who could only roll her eyes. "I've been too busy yelling at him," Joan said, "to fill him in on everything. Although he did let Marcus know he wasn't going to be left out." She reached over and took his hand. He didn't let go.

"So...does this mean...?" She waited for her friend to finish her sentence. Joan and Max just looked at her. "For crying out loud," Sierra groaned, "are you pregnant, or not?"

"Oh, that," Joan grinned at her friend's frustration. "No. And yes." Sierra reached over and picked up the small plastic water pitcher - and held it over Max's head. "Someone better start talking - or the boy toy here takes a shower."

"Hey," Max protested, "you can't call me that, we're the same age."

"You're ten years younger than your girlfriend, so yeah, I can call you whatever I want."

"Watch yourself, you're talking about the woman I love, who happens to be my fiancé."

Sierra mouth dropped open. Joan hugged her. "No, I'm not pregnant. Turns out that pond I fell into wasn't fit for human consumption, some kind of bacteria thing. And, yes, Max and I have decided to start trying to become pregnant. And, yes, we are getting married." Fresh tears welled in Joan's eyes. "And I'm hoping-"

"We're hoping," Max interjected.

"Okay, we're hoping you'll be my maid of honor."

“Technically, she’ll be your matron of honor.” Max interjected, again.

Sierra dropped the water pitcher and hugged her friend tightly. "I'm so happy for you!"

"Hey! That’s cold!" Max yelped, as the pitcher landed in his lap. "Watch the stitches." He swatted it to the floor as a large wet spot spread across his sheet. No one noticed.

"Finally." The deep voice boomed from the doorway, catching Joan's attention. In three long strides, Charles Henry had his arms wrapped around his cousin. Marcus walked into the room too, a to-go tray of coffee in one hand and a bag of pastry in the other. Sierra met him at the door smiling.

"What did I miss?" Marcus asked. "Doesn't matter...turn up the volume on the TV, quick. There's a special News update. He handed a coffee to Sierra. "Take this,” he took one for himself and set the rest on the bed stand. "I found a Starbucks next door."

Joan turned up the sound. The screen showed Willow's house, all lit up, and a crowd of people in front of it. The scene showed police cars, plus an ambulance with its lights flashing. They could hear a news reporter, standing on the sidewalk, giving a running commentary. "Breaking news - the suspect of all the trouble in downtown Vancouver these last three days, is also a murder suspect. Ms. Symms, in an attempt to avoid our questions jumped off the porch that you see on your screen and ran to the backyard. Hoping, more than likely, to hide in the dark. Unfortunately for her, the root cellar doors were open, and she fell in, breaking her leg in the process. She is currently being transferred to a hospital. More details to come, back to you, Bob." Joan turned it off. For a few moments everyone was quiet.

"Wow," Sierra said, breaking the silence. "That's karma for you. I hope she gets what she deserves."

Charles Henry closed his eyes tightly as tears traced down his cheeks. "It's not that simple." Everyone watched him, waiting quietly. "Willow fell down the stairs and Amelia were arguing. Amelia wanted to buy the property to keep the yoga studio open. Willow didn't want to do that. Amelia swears it was an accident, and called for an ambulance."

"Wait, you're saying Gwendolyn is innocent?" Joan asked. "But she's so horrible."

"I didn't say she was innocent," Charles Henry said. "The flash drive shows the authorities all the information they need." He stopped to catch his breath. He'd keep the scene of Gwendolyn finding Willow at the bottom of the stairs taking her earrings, plus the last scene of Willow's death, to himself. He mopped his face with a tissue, his tears flowing now. "And then she walked away from Willow's body with a smile on her face."

Stunned, Joan and Sierra rushed forward to hug Charles Henry. Max and Marcus looked at each other and shook their heads. Joan's cousin broke the hugging first. "Enough, enough, let's think of the positive things here." He grabbed a coffee.

Sierra turned to her husband. "Max and Joan are engaged."

"Yo, Marcus," Max was all smiles, a pile of wet sheets on the floor and a dry blanket covering his legs. "I'm getting married. If I'd known all I had to do was get stabbed, I'd have done it two years ago."

Charles Henry passed the other two coffees to Max and Joan. He cleared his throat and waited a moment, wanting their full attention. He raised his cup to make a toast. "To justice found for my beloved Willow."

Joan grabbed Sierra and hugged her. "We did it, we found justice for Willow. And I couldn't have done it without you." She turned and looked at Marcus. "Is this how you two felt? When you helped that Irish shopkeeper, Patrick? Did you feel satisfied?"

"Not really." Sierra put her arm around Marcus. "First, we felt sad, Patrick had lost a good friend. And then, we were very thankful we still had each other."

"I'm adding to your toast, Charles," Marcus said. "To love found, for Max and Joan. And for their wedding, may they be blessed." Amid tears and laughter everyone lifted their cups and sipped.

He had to ask. "So, when and where is this wedding going to take place?" Inwardly, Marcus cringed. Knowing Joan's exotic tastes, he expected to hear about camels in Marrakesh, or penguins in Antarctica, or hot air balloons over the plains of Africa.

"Well," Joan said, as Max smiled. "We want to get married this coming mid- December, in San Francisco at the Dickens Christmas Fair." She turned to Sierra and Marcus. "It's an amazing holiday event that's been growing for over thirty years. It's held at the Cow Palace."

"Wow. Nice choice. Quite the destination." Marcus couldn't stop smiling. "I can see this being fun." Relief flooded through his body and he couldn't resist whispering in Sierra's ear. "This actually sounds safe. What can possibly happen at a Christmas Fair?"

A Mermaid's Tears

The metal screen door slammed in the warm twilight and the air hung heavy and sweet, filled with the droning whine of insects. Isa Andrews sighed and swatted at mosquitoes as she bee lined to the truck, her sandals slapping against the cracked sidewalk. Two more trips carrying boxes from the cab of the U-Haul truck and she'd be done. Anxious to claim her sister's place as her own, she crawled into the cab and grabbed the lawn ornament she'd purchased earlier that day.

Carefully setting it down in the scrub grass near the trailer, Isa stood back and studied her surroundings. The small trailer park showed its age. The two dozen doublewides, faded and worn, had withstood years of hot blistering sun, salty ocean air, and countless storms.

Isa glanced over at her neighbor's yard, another empty piece of tired grass that pretty much matched her sister's. Bushes and trees abounded but no fun things like plastic pink flamingos or sparkly sun catchers appeared anywhere. Sheesh, she figured Florida would be full of them. She bent over and adjusted her first attempt at home ownership, sticking the legs of the small plastic animal firmly into the soft soil. It stood on the edge of the grass near the bushes at the back of the trailer, reminding her of the Florida Key deer she'd heard about on the drive down from New York. Small, and covered with fake fuzzy tan fur with large chocolate brown eyes, it looked very lifelike, brightening up the small piece of grass her sister called a yard.

A slow-moving creek hidden by overgrown shrubbery bordered the backyard, twenty feet from the two-bedroom trailer butting up against the cracked driveway and gravel road at the front. Old Live Oak trees blocked the view of the ocean that lay a mere half mile away just on the other side of the highway. She slapped at another mosquito, trying to ignore the sweat trickling down between her shoulder blades. She was 'glistening', as her sister Kate would write in her poetry.

At the moment, she'd have to disagree. Glistening was the afterglow on the skin after having fabulous hot sex with your man. Unpacking a U Haul truck in the hot, muggy Florida Keys in August didn't come anywhere close. Isa frowned; in fact, she hadn't been close to glistening for almost a year. And right now, all she wanted was a shower – a long, leisurely, tepid shower. But first, pictures, that's what she needed. Determined to start a new photo journal, it was a must to document her first night at what would be her home away from home for the next four months.

Grabbing her Nikon from the driver's seat she focused and shot the purple gold evening sky, the last dredges of daylight smudged in color waiting for the stars to appear. Checking her flash, she turned to photograph the new lawn ornament Little Bubba, as she'd named the little deer, but the lawn was empty. He was gone.

She glanced over at the porch. Nothing there. Now wait a minute, she wasn't that forgetful. It was fake, it couldn't move itself, so where did it go? A soft sound caught her ears and the hairs on the back of her neck stood up. She turned slowly to face a huge alligator sitting in the grass, the Key deer in his mouth. She froze, adrenalin bursting in her heart, fizzing through her brain and down to her toes. For several moments she forgot to breathe.

The alligator sat there as if waiting. Slowly it chewed on the hard plastic and fuzzy fabric, rolling it around against its teeth; his prey's sightless brown eyes bulging from between his mammoth jaws. Isa almost felt sorry for the huge beast because it actually looked confused. What a rude surprise for him, tasting cold plastic instead of warm flesh and hot blood. Slowly she moved her camera to face him. Carefully, steadily, she pressed the button. God bless instant focus she thought. So far, so good. A bright flash filled the yard with light. Cold, dead eyes swiveled up and locked onto hers. Uh-oh.

He hadn't moved, but suddenly the air between them radiated anger and great danger. Barely realizing the screams she heard were hers, she jumped onto the wooden porch and in one fluid motion opened her screen door and threw herself into the trailer. Trying to catch her breath she watched out the kitchen window as the alligator casually crawled along the grass towards the bushes lining the creek. He turned his great head, his unblinking eyes finding hers, the Key Deer still in his mouth. His body language spoke loudly. *"I'll be back."* He turned and slithered into the water.

Trembling, Isa believed he would.

Praise for Sylissa Franklin's other novels

Emerald Wiles

(the 1st book in Sierra Scott mystery series)

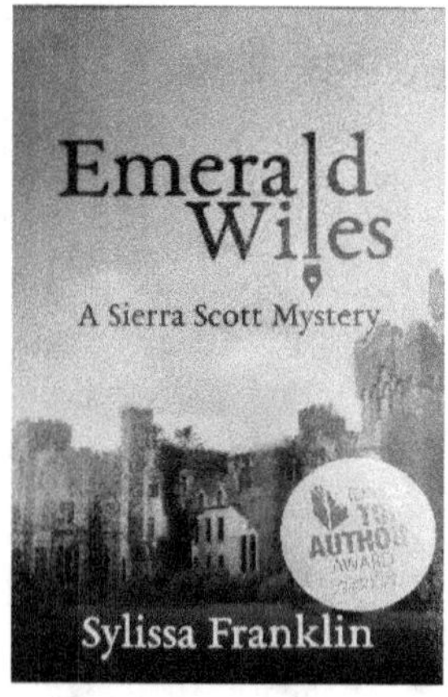

Helen Clark... **"My new favorite author!"**

"I can't wait to read Sylissa's next book. This one had me glued the whole time. Best mystery I've read in a long time. I highly recommend this book. You've gotta read it! I'm hooked!"

Chrystal Allen ... **"Page turner"**

"Great read. Enough edge to make it suspenseful but not too scary. I can't wait to read the next in the series."

Pearls...for Better or for Worse

(the 3rd book in Sierra Scott mystery series)

KATZ... **"Intriguing"**

"Good job! Insightful and well planned. Looking forward to the next book. Loved the locals. You just can't keep Sierra down."

Phil Sander... **"the characters stay true from one of Sylissa's books to the next adventure."**

"I love easy reading mystery books. They really hold my attention."

A Mermaid's Tears

(stand-alone Romantic Suspense)

Lee Murray...**"Perfect Escapism!"**

"Romance doesn't feature strongly in my reading choices, but this was definitely worth making the switch because when a book's heroine runs into both a cantankerous crocodile and a swarthy pirate in the first chapter, there's a good bet it'll be a winner... An entertaining read with a gripping finale that really romps along, A Mermaid's Tears is perfect escapism."

M. Fechter ... **"Fun romantic adventure with a fish-out-of-water heroine and a pirate hero."**

"Isa has moved to the Florida Keys when her life in NYC takes a turn for the worse. She meets up with an alligator who doesn't appreciate her attempt to beautify her yard, a neighbor who watches her all the time, and the sexiest history teacher in, well, history. It's a fun, twisty adventure including diving, sharks, vandalism and kidnapping. It definitely kept me turning the pages!"

About the Author, Sylissa Franklin

Sylissa blends the genres of mystery and suspense, with a touch of romance. She champions the underdog as she writes about ordinary people, caught up in extraordinary circumstances. Then, she lets the sparks fly. Her protagonists are highly relatable, but she makes sure her antagonists are not flat, 2-D caricatures. Sometimes they're as complicated as they are evil.

This avid writer, traveler, art collector, and nature lover is American, born in the UK. She lived for a time in Germany, France, and numerous places all across the United States, before settling in Boise, Idaho. Recently heeding her inner Mermaid, she picked up her notebook, sold her home, and moved to the Garden Isle, in the State of Hawai'i.

Loving to travel as much as she enjoys 'talking story', she weaves international destinations into her books, making the locations just as important as her characters. Sylissa is a huge dog lover (literally), having owned both Saint Bernards and Great Danes. She's excited to have added a Blue Merle Great Dane puppy to her household. His eyes are as blue as the ocean that stretches out in every direction from her tropical island paradise. Sylissa's eyes also light up, in the presence of bling, especially in the form of jewelry.

Her Cozy Mystery books and stand-alone novels have garnered national notoriety, awards, and prizes. Her very first published novel was a Golden Heart Finalist in Contemporary Romance. Some of her short stories have been selected for inclusion in some Top 10 anthologies.

Sylissa has been on panels at various writers' conferences, loves to meet her fans at book signings, holds educational seminars about writing, and speaking. She has co-hosted 'AutoCrit' live video classes for writers focusing on 'NaNoWriMo' (National Novel Writing Month) challenge.

Sylissa seldom passes up an opportunity to talk about writing.

Mahalo and Aloha.

Sylissa's Kindle eBooks and paperbacks are available through Amazon.

SYLISSA.COM is this author's web page. Learn more about her, and coordinate book signings, mentoring, crewing of conference panels, cruises and co-hosting both writing and speaking related events.

Shout-outs to:

AutoCrit online manuscript editing site: AUTOCRIT.COM

FayeFayeDesigns creates Sylissa's marvelous book covers: FIVERR.COM/FAYEFAYEDESIGNS

www.ingramcontent.com/pod-product-compliance
Lightning Source LLC
Chambersburg PA
CBHW070515260626
47161CB00004B/1553

* 9 7 8 0 9 9 9 4 8 2 5 0 6 *